Hexes & Heroes

A CASTLE POINT WITCH SERIES BOOK 3

TAMMY TYREE

Shale Empire Press

TAMMY TYREE

HEXES
AND
HEROES

A CASTLE POINT WITCH SERIES
BOOK 3

978-1-7389792-9-5 Hexes & Hero'sDigital E-Book

978-1-7389792-8-8 Hexes & Hero's Paperback

978-1-7389792-7-1 Hexes & Hero's Large Print

978-1-7389792-6-4 Hexes & Hero's Audio Book

Any references to historical events, real people, or places are fictitious. Names, characters, and places are products of the author's imagination.

Front cover image by Mibl Art

Book designed with Vellum

First printing edition 2023

Shale Empire Press

shaleempire@gmail.com

www.tammytyreebooks.com

For C
Keep fighting your demons
I love you

ACKNOWLEDGMENTS

To my dear readers, your unwavering support and encouragement have been the guiding stars in this creative odyssey. Your insightful reviews and heartwarming feedback have fueled the fires of my inspiration, burning brightly, even during moments of doubt.

As this chapter of our journey comes to a close, I eagerly anticipate the new tales that await us. Thank you for being an integral part of this magical experience. Your enthusiasm and love for Alexandra's world have delighted every written word.

Here's to the adventures and the stories yet to be told.

With heartfelt gratitude,
Tammy Tyree

AUTHOR'S NOTE

Like my other books in this series, this is a fiction work.
The demons, however, are real.

PROLOGUE

The History of the Demon, Murder.

According to the Testament of Solomon, many of the demons in Solomon's encounters are of Greek, Egyptian, Jewish, Christian, Arabic, and other traditions.

The majority of the testament consists of Solomon's interviews with the demons, some of which are grotesque, including one that has no head.

"Murder" is the headless demon Solomon refers to. One who sees through his breasts and speaks with the voice taken over from his victims. The Testament states that Murder is summoned to appear before King Solomon. He has no head, and he tries to get one by devouring the heads of his victims.

Murder grabs heads, cuts them off, and attaches them to himself.

A real prize, would you agree?

And we had the displeasure of meeting him, as you'll see within the following pages...

Hang on to your heads, people.
Things are about to get weird...

ALEXANDRA Heale

CHAPTER
ONE

ALEXANDRA

The sun poked my eyelids like a persistent alarm clock, waking me up with a not-so-gentle nudge. I sprawled out, feeling the warm rays creep through a tiny opening in the fancy velvet curtains. With a groggy stretch, I kicked off the comfy quilt and exited the flouncy bed. My feet hit the cold stone floor, and I quickly hopped into my slippers, shivering.

I shuffled to the window; my nightdress—what used to be Evelyn of Cumbria's, found in a dusty cedar chest in this bedroom with her other 17th-century garb—billowed around me as I tugged open the heavy drapes. The view outside was epic—Castle Point, the town, and the endless ocean. Sunlight glinted off a snowy blanket covering everything.

"Good morning, brave new world," I croaked, still half-asleep.

My new dig, Castle Dagon, was this crazy medieval

fortress on a cliff. It had this wild combination of old-school castle torment, terror vibes, and modern gadgets.

Oh, and don't forget the magic, secrets, and danger.

I am living the dream.

Being the Dagon Queen meant I was smack in that craziness. I'm a witch, but my powers got jacked, and now I'm stuck with these creepy Dagon powers and Witch Hunters lurking in the shadows, itching for a witch-hunting party. I might've lost my witchy powers to their dead boss, Earl Dagon, but I'm not letting them win.

Nope, I own them.

At least, that's what I kept telling myself.

Earl Dagon—that drama king—made me queen at a Witch Hunter ceremony. I guess being dead doesn't stop you from having a thing for power. Thanks to him, I'm straddling two worlds like a circus performer.

From the other side, Earl Dagon knew I'd reincarnated as a witch. So, he ordered a batch of possessed, demonic Hench-nuns to strip my witchy powers the night of my thirty-eighth birthday—the same age he'd torched me as Evelyn of Cumbria back in the day. I had to tap into my ancestral Dagon mojo to escape that firepit.

Once free, I let those Dagon powers loose, just like Earl wanted. If he couldn't have me as Evelyn from the 1600s or Alexandra from today, he'd make me *his* kind of Dagon.

Now, I've got this title I loathe, a castle I never wanted and a legacy I could do without.

But, hey, it's all about embracing the drama, right?

So, I might be the Queen of the Witch Hunters, but trust me, they're not throwing me a party. I told Sheriff Gordon Roberts, the Witch Hunter High Commander, to send an official order telling the hunters to cool it with the witch hunts. No more power-stripping ceremonies for witches like me and my friend Penny. Not that they've had much luck finding a witch in the past fifty years.

Witches are ninja-level at hiding.

But my orders had the opposite effect.

Witch Hunters worldwide went into overdrive, which meant the secret witch society had to stay even more secret. And my Dagon powers were useless against them. Earl Dagon seemed to want his honey and peanut butter, too. Put his long-lost love in command...over no one.

I could use my powers to threaten them, but only those who took the threat seriously. The rest served up the age-old misogyny on a vast, Dagon-forged platter.

Just freaking fabulous.

Now, I must figure out how to stop the hunters and end their reign of terror.

I gazed at the horizon where the sea met the sky, thinking about Blake. He's been MIA since the night I became castle queen weeks ago. Despite my efforts, there was no trace of him. His absence was like a heavy weight on my heart.

I remembered the last time we were together—sparks flying when we kissed, his strong arms around me. We weren't officially a couple, but that kiss was etched in my memory, making Blake's disappearance even more chal-lenging.

I turned to the mirror, addressing my reflection as I did daily. "Alexandra Heale, you're a force to be reckoned with." My long, dark hair framed my face just right, and my green eyes held more secrets than a gossip column. I was ready for whatever craziness came my way.

At least, that's what I kept telling myself.

I pulled at the ash-filled vial earring of my mentor, Cressy's ashes dangling from my left lobe. The comforting tug calmed my nerves and connected me to my late mentor.

"Ah, the classic self-pep talk," a voice quipped from the corner of the room. *"Never gets old."* It was Blackjack, my sassy black feline familiar. We had this mind-link thing, so we didn't need words to chat. He strutted over, sunlight glossing his sleek fur to an ebony shine. ."*Sleep well,* Your Highness?" he quipped in his usual sarcastic tone, giving a little bow.

"Yeah," I replied, "and I'm feeling... optimistic...and stuff."

"Optimistic?" Blackjack teased, jumping onto the windowsill. *"Now, that's a plot twist. What's got you feeling all hopeful 'and stuff'?"*

"Maybe it's the sunshine, or maybe it's just a gut feeling," I pondered, checking out the town below. "But I believe we're close to getting my witchy powers back and kicking Witch Hunters to the curb."

"Big words," Blackjack purred, stretching lazily. *"But let's hope you're not just serving up some wishful thinking."*

"Trust me," I scratched my familiar behind the ears, then pulled my hand away as darts of Dagon heat prickled my palm.

"Easy, tiger. Don't burn the castle down with all that ferocity," Blackjack teased, flicking his tail at me. *"I enjoy living here. I have a staff of minions catering to my every whim and a castle full of mice to prey upon. Life is good."*

"Hilarious," I replied dryly, rolling my eyes. "And also, ew. But I'm serious, Blackjack. I need to figure this out."

"Of course, Your Highness," he responded, his green eyes locking onto mine. *"And we'll do it together. We'll find that spell and get your powers back. And maybe... just maybe, we'll find the big doofus sheriff along the way. Although I've never*

understood what you see in that man, I suppose I can support your quest to find him."

"Alrighty, let's do it," I declared, ignoring his smirky attitude. I tossed the nightdress onto the bed, pulled on my usual fashion of late—sweats—and left the room with Blackjack in tow, a sputter of kitty farts escaping his back end as he trotted down the stone stairs of our castle wing. I plugged my nose and rushed down the steps, overtaking the stinky brat.

Coffee is calling.

It was definitely time for a caramel macchiato with extra foam.

After that, I'd tackle whatever challenges came my way with a dash of courage, a sprinkle of cunning, and, of course, a good dose of caffeine.

"Focus, Alex," I scolded myself. My macchiato foam art attempts were epic failures. Instead of a cat, I'd crafted what looked like a soggy rat. I gave up and took a long swig of my extra-creamy goodness.

"Can I make your coffee for you, my lady?" Malcolm, my butler and chief-of-staff, appeared out of nowhere like he had teleportation powers.

I jumped, spilling some of my coffee. Malcolm quickly mopped at the mess with a dishrag. "Uh, no, thanks, Malcolm, I can manage," I replied with a grin, taking another gulp of my morning catastrophe.

Malcolm nodded and departed. The guy was a tall, stoic figure with the charisma of Lurch from the Addams Family. He'd worked closely with the former museum curator, but I couldn't recall ever seeing him at work in the castle when it was a museum. Still, his resume checked out, and when I called Mr. Fellows for a reference, he had given him a glowing recommendation, so I'd taken him on.

I'd shut down the museum part of the castle when I moved in and gave Mr. Fellows a golden parachute so he could retire in style. I'd kept most of the other staff on payroll, with some taking a leave of absence and others shuffled into different roles. Maintaining this massive castle and its gardens was no small feat, especially with winter approaching.

My thoughts veered back to The Book of the Order of Witch Hunters: that ancient tome holding the secret to reclaiming my powers...I hoped. Sheriff Roberts said no such spell existed within the book, but I refused to take his word for it. Determination surged within me like a fire-cracker. I was dead set on cracking the cryptic code concealed within its pages. Nothing could deter me. With sheer stubbornness as my co-pilot, I left the kitchen and headed into Castle Dagon's grand hall.

Despite the infusion of caffeine into my veins, I already felt tired.

Keeping the determination dialed high was an exhausting task.

Walking, I felt the gravity of my mission to regain my stolen powers. But I couldn't let the hunters win. I would decode The Book and restore my abilities, no matter what.

"Morning, Alex!" Teddy's cheerful voice echoed from what used to be Mr. Fellows' enormous office as I passed by. "Ready to dive into some more code-breaking fun?"

"Absolutely," I replied, my smile not quite making it to my eyes. "I'm not resting until I get my powers back."

"Good on you, boss," Teddy said, her brown eyes oozing warmth and encouragement. She was hard at work, grinding herbs like a seasoned pro to whip up one of her potent teas for my shop, Castle Point Apothecary. Today, Teddy had ditched her usual magically induced glam look of purple hair and tattoos. Her loyal hellhounds lounged at her feet in their natural splendor.

Those hellhounds were big softies, just like Teddy. Despite their gnashing teeth, gray scaling skin, and size, they were slobbery puppies rather than fearsome beasts, and loyal to a fault. That's why I'd invited Teddy and her crew to move into the castle with me. They deserved the space, and I relished their company and the extra protection.

"Maybe today will be our lucky day," I mused, stepping into the massive library and cradling The Book. My fingers traced its spine, and I couldn't help but feel a surge of determination.

Today, I was going to make progress.

CHAPTER

TWO

BLAKE

The memory crashed over me like a hurricane, swirling and pulling me into its chaotic vortex. The hood over my head shrouded my senses in the oppressive darkness. My heart raced, adrenaline coursing through my veins, and I could almost smell my fear. The anticipation hung heavy as I waited, hooded, for what would come next.

Someone yanked the hood off my head. A rush of cool air hit my face, carrying the scent of gasoline.

I was in a wheelchair, in a garage, in nowhere land.

Two blurry figures stood in the dim light. As they approached, unmistakable recognition coursed through my veins with the speed of a thousand horses.

"Mom? Dad?" I croaked, disbelief and shock flooding my senses. Their faces loomed before me, and I could smell the faintest traces of their familiar scents. My heart pounded as I inhaled Mom's cinnamon and bergamot fragrance, mingled with Dad's earthy cologne.

Mom couldn't contain herself and rushed forward, her perfume enveloping me as she embraced me. I sat bound to a chair, the rough texture of the ropes digging into my skin as her scent engulfed me. I could taste the saltiness of tears mingling with her perfume as she wiped her face, her fingers warm against my cheeks. She smelled just as I remembered.

"My boy," Dad said gruffly, embracing us both. His neatly trimmed beard scratched my cheek just like when I was little. I could feel the warmth of their bodies as they hugged me, and my skin tingled with the sensation.

They were real. The world felt vivid and surreal, and I couldn't fathom this miraculous reunion. Mom untied the ropes around my ankles, the fibers sliding against my skin, leaving an impression of their roughness. Dad untied my hands, and I could feel the slight sting as circulation returned.

My parents were alive.

It was as if I could touch the reality of their presence. I was overwhelmed by a whirlwind of happiness, confusion, and an inexplicable yearning for a family. I thought I'd lost forever.

But I needed answers, and fast.

AFTER THE EMOTIONAL REUNION, I found myself on the porch of Magma's home, only a few hours from Castle Point. The old magnolia trees, their leaves now absent in the early winter chill, surrounded the weathered farmhouse. I sipped on a hot chocolate laced with Bourbon that Magma had prepared, the warmth easing my nerves. Steam curled around my face, carrying the rich aroma of chocolate and the faint hint of whiskey. The whipped topping on the hot chocolate was thick and creamy, its sweet scent teasing my senses.

Thoughts of Alexandra tugged at my mind, her image vivid in my memory. Samhain had just ended—along with Alex's thirty-eight birthday—and I did not know if she escaped the demonic nun's torment or was lying six feet under the frosty ground.

Or worse, if there could be one. Suppose they burned her—alive—on the castle pyre.

I shook my head, pushing the thought away and choosing to think she was alive, well, and had escaped to the shadows of the underworld, much like my parents did so many years ago. I wished I could tell her everything that had happened. But I knew I needed to wait. Mom and Dad still had much to answer for, and I wasn't leaving until their entire story was told. I closed my eyes and could almost hear the soft rustle of her hair and the delicate sound of her laughter in the late fall air.

"Blake, there's so much we need to tell you," my father's approach broke my reverie. He settled on the porch swing with a cup of hot chocolate, his voice heavy with regret. Mom joined us on the porch, wrapping me in a knitted blanket before sitting beside Dad on the porch swing, snugging a second blanket over their knees.

I cleared my throat. "That was you on the beach. I was sitting in my squad car, napping after a long night. I thought I was delirious from lack of sleep, seeing things, but it was you." I said, peering at my dad.

"Yes, it was me, Son. We were staying close. We knew we needed to take you."

I shook my head. "Why? And why *kidnap* me? Couldn't

you just come to see me? Also, why has everyone lied to me about your death all these years?"

Dad ran a hand through his short-cropped hair.

Just like I do.

"Like I said. We have a lot to tell you, Son."

"I'm listening."

Dad took a deep breath and blew it out hard. "I hardly know where to start."

"From the beginning, seems like a good place," I stated, somewhat sarcastically.

He nodded. "We had to fake our deaths to protect you and ourselves,"

My throat worked. "Protect me? From what?"

Dad's expression darkened. "From the death threats. From the truth."

I ran a hand through my hair, mirroring my father's mannerisms, and exhaled an exasperated breath. "Dad. Enough of the cloak-and-dagger bullshit. I'm a grown man. I can take it. Just tell me, what the hell is going on?"

Dad held his mug in both hands, permissively glancing at Mom, who nodded in silent agreement.

"We're witches, Son. As are you."

My mouth fell open, a dribble of chocolate spilling onto my scruffy chin.

Witches? Us? Me?

It couldn't be.

"No." I shook my head. "That can't be true. You were a Witch Hunter. I'm a Witch Hunter."

Mom nodded. "We bound your powers as a babe to keep you safe. We had to fake our deaths when you were eighteen to protect you. The Witch Hunters—or someone —was closing in on us."

"Bind my powers? Closing in on us? What does that mean?" My voice cracked.

Dad continued. "Someone found out what I am. We assume it was someone within the Order. Somehow, they discovered I'd infiltrated them as a spy." His eyes flashed with anger. "I worked my way up to High Commander so I could take them down from the inside, dismantle them piece by piece. The death threats were coming in heavy and hot. We had to fake our deaths and disappear to protect you and stay alive so we could keep working on a way to take them down."

My body went weak. It was too much to take in all at once.

Witches, powers, Witch Hunters—my entire world turned upside down. "Impossible," I whispered, shaking my head, then searching for the closest available spot to release the contents of my stomach as it roiled. Slapping a hand over my mouth, I stood up. My stomach roiled again with...disgust? Disbelief?

But deeper down, below the yawning threat of losing yesterday's leftover pizza, something inside me stirred. A dormant knowing that had been bound and hidden for my protection, perhaps? I sat down hard.

Mom got up from the swing and crouched beside me; her eyes searched my face, tears glistening. "We had to keep you safe, Blake. We had to keep everyone safe. I know this is a shock, sweetheart. But we're together again now..." she rambled on.

As I listened, anger and betrayal fought for dominance within me. How could they have left me alone all those years, letting me think they were dead? Why hadn't I sensed the truth sooner? If, at my core, I'm a witch, then I should've been able to sense who I was, wouldn't I?

"Your powers had been bound, Son," my father said. I wondered if he had been reading my thoughts, then decided that was likely. "We had to protect you. I hadn't counted on you following in my footsteps and becoming a Witch Hunter. I realize it's because you didn't know the truth, but it wasn't something I'd expected but should have. Because we were so close to Gordon, naturally, he would enlist you into the Order." Dad was referring to Gordon Roberts, the Sheriff...and one of Dad's closest friends, or so I thought. "I regret not being able to tell you— to protect you from the false beliefs the Order has held sacred for over 400 years."

"Why now? What's happening that made you think kidnapping me was a good plan?"

Dad looked at me sheepishly. "Sorry about that, Son. But we weren't—aren't—sure where your loyalties lie. If we had exposed ourselves to you on *your* turf, we risked being arrested...or worse..."

I pursed my lips, looking into my mug of dwindling hot chocolate. "You're my parents. Did you *really* think I could turn on you? I wouldn't have known about the witch thing unless you told me..." my head throbbed.

"Son, whoever tried to kill us twenty years ago could still be out there. We couldn't risk alerting you or anyone else to our truth. We had to bring you back here, far away from the central hub of hunter activity."

Mom leaned forward. "You understand, don't you, Blake? This was the only way."

I looked into her eyes, then to Dad's, watching tears form and spill over onto cheeks I hadn't kissed for twenty years. I'd forgotten what their eyes looked like. I had forgotten how they smelled, hugged, and loved me. A deep, aching hole in my heart was slowly filling. "Of course, I understand. But you still haven't answered me. Why now?"

Dad leaned forward, placing his mug on the table, his elbows on his knees, and rubbed his hands together. "They alerted us to the Witch Hunter's capture of Alexandra Heale and her friend, Penny."

I bowed my head. "That was my fault; I was trying to fix it when you took me."

Dad's eyebrows lifted, but he went on. "We knew you were the one who turned them in—sort of—but we didn't know you were trying to amend the situation. We didn't want you to be the one to strip them of their powers. To take their lives. We knew our son could never live with that if he were still the wonderful son we left behind." A tear slipped down Dad's cheek, its wet trail glistening in the approaching moonlight.

"We thought," my mom spoke softly, "that it was time you knew who you really were. That perhaps, in knowing, we could work together...to..."

"End the hunters." I finished her sentence.

She nodded. "Yes. Your destiny was never to be a Witch Hunter, Son. You've always been a witch and didn't know it."

"But now it's time to release your powers. You have a destiny to fulfill." Dad wiped his face with his hand.

"A *destiny*? What destiny? And who did this to us?" I demanded, clenching my fists. "Who wants us dead?"

"We don't know," my mother admitted, her voice barely a whisper. "But we suspect it's someone close to us— someone who has likely been hiding in plain sight all this time."

I shook my head no. It couldn't be. "Gordon?"

"We don't know, Son. It could be Gordon, Jeff Deibert,

or any of the hunters who were once in my command. All we know is we must be careful," my father warned, his brown eyes dark with concern. "This person—or people—are cunning and ruthless. They'll stop at nothing to destroy us and anyone connected to us. We have to end this, Son. We have to fight back."

"Wait, how did you know I was responsible for Penny and Alex's..." I was about to say 'death' but couldn't let the word cross my lips. "...hunter-napping?"

"We are part of the underground, Blake. Witches have been infiltrating the Order, the police force, you name it, for decades. Getting information and keeping tabs on you for the past twenty years has been pretty easy."

A shiver ran through me. Who's our friend? Who's our enemy? The lines seemed so blurred. "This is a lot to take in..."

"We'll help you through all of this, Blake. We'll unbind your powers and teach you about your...gifts..." Mom continued.

Wait. Gifts?

I had gifts?

I had gifts!

A cool fountain of truth and understanding washed over me.

Alexandra was a witch. Someone I had sworn to hate, to...kill. Yet I couldn't. Maybe it was because I had fallen for Alexandra, but...perhaps...it was because I knew I was one of 'them' deep down. I could imagine Alexandra laughing at me, the Dagon-loving, witch-hating...*witch*. I could visualize her long black hair rustling down her back as laughter burst from her perfect lips.

The lips I just had to kiss again and be kissed by.

If she's even alive to do so.

Determination settled in my chest like a stone about to fall from an endless cliff. I knew what I had to do - I would unmask the traitor and protect my family, friends, and Alexandra - the woman I loved and hoped was still alive.

"Teach me," I said, my voice steady and robust. "Teach me how to embrace my powers and put an end to this once and for all."

A frosty wind picked up, sending a shiver down my spine. Dark clouds loomed on the horizon, flickering with a silent winter storm. The animals and forest in and around the farm fell quiet—holding their breath.

There was a storm coming in more ways than one. Whoever nearly killed my parents was still out there. Once my parents unbound my magic, they would surely sense it... and they'd be coming for blood. For all our sakes, I needed to be ready for the fight ahead.

Something wicked this way comes.

And I feared Alexandra would be caught in the crossfire.

THE SUN DIPPED low in the sky, casting a golden hue over Magma's home as I sat under the blanket on the porch long after my parents and Magma went to bed. The old Crone had been keeping my parents safe for two decades, and now it was time for me to face my destiny. My fingers traced the worn wood of the railing, feeling its grooves and imperfections as I thought about the immense task ahead.

In the distance, I could smell the enticing scent of roses from Magma's garden, still red and blooming despite the pre-winter chill. The calming aroma couldn't quite chase away the storm of emotions within me.

The scent reminded me of Alexandra.

As much as I wanted to reach out to her, find her, and see if she was even alive—I knew I couldn't—not until after the unbinding ceremony, and I'd had some time to practice with my powers. The thought of facing off against an unknown enemy filled me with dread and determination.

"Blake?" Magma's voice carried softly through the evening air, her tone gentle but firm.

I turned on hearing my name. "Magma. I thought you'd gone to bed." I smiled at the slightly hunched, silver-haired, ageless beauty. She stayed with us late into the evening, talking and reminiscing about the past twenty years.

She walked across the porch, her dressing gown blowing in the burgeoning wind, her long, wavy gray hair billowing behind her. "You cannot let your thoughts consume you, boy. Control your emotions, or they will control you."

I looked down at her, taking in her wise eyes and weathered features. She was right, of course. I needed to focus on the task at hand. "Thank you, Magma," I replied, forcing a smile. "It's hard not being able to tell Alex everything that's going on. I don't even know if she survived."

"Oh, don't think such thoughts. Practice patience, dear boy," she counseled, her eyes twinkling with understanding. "Once we have performed the unbinding ceremony and you've learned to harness your powers, you can face this threat together."

My heart ached at the mention of Alexandra, the woman who had become my rock in these turbulent times. I longed to share my burden with her, but I knew doing so would only place her in greater danger.

"When can we begin the ceremony?" I asked, stepping toward her, wrapping my arm around her slight shoulders, and leading her toward the door. My legs quivered, but I forced myself to relax.

Her voice filled with quiet resolve. "Tomorrow night, we unbind your powers and set you on the path to fulfilling your destiny."

As we stepped into the warm glow of Magma's home, I couldn't help but feel a strange mixture of fear and excitement coursing through my veins. The road ahead was steeped in danger and secrecy, but I knew I had no choice but to walk it if I hoped to protect those I loved.

With each step I took, I tried to push thoughts of Alexandra from my mind, focusing instead on the unbinding ceremony that would take place.

Little did I know that this would begin a journey that would test my strength, loyalty, and love in ways I never imagined.

THREE

ALEXANDRA

I took a deep breath, inhaling the scent of ancient stone and lingering sage that filled the castle. Large, ancient books about the Witch Hunters from the castle library shelves spread around the room. Penny, Teddy, and I had been poring over the tomes, trying to find a key to unlocking the ancient language, but so far, nothing. Sheriff Roberts and his deputies were no closer to finding a hunter elder who understood and could interpret the old script—the elders claimed that even if they *could* interpret the text, they wouldn't help *a witch.*

At least, that's what he told me they said.

And I couldn't force them or even blame them for it. As we all knew, the world turned upside-down when the dead Earl Dagon crowned me queen. I'd likely react the same way if in their shoes.

So, Teddy, Penny, and I were on our own, poring over old books and history like it was our new day job.

We had even discovered Earl Dagon's journals—accidentally on one of Penny and Teddy's hide-and-seek hunts through the castle—but the personal thoughts of the late Earl gave nothing away.

Reading about our history together, as Earl Dagon and Evelyn of Cumbria, was as enlightening as it was sickening. I had to keep my dark, red-hot Dagon heat from exploding the entire library the more I read his horrific account of burning Evelyn—me—on the pyre. I pulled on the small vial earring and flipped through ancient text pages.

"Woman," whispered a voice in my mind, snapping me out of my reverie, *"you've been at this for hours. It's time to take a break."*

I closed The Book with a sigh, my tired eyes straining to look through the curved library window and the endless expanse of the sea. "You're right, Blackjack," I admitted to my familiar, who lounged on the desk beside me. His green eyes gleamed with amusement as he regarded me through the dusky afternoon light.

"Of course I'm right," he replied smugly, his tail flicking back and forth. *"When have I ever been wrong?"*

I couldn't help but chuckle at his arrogance. "Let's not get carried away now."

"Stubborn as ever," he teased, but I could feel the warmth of his concern through our mental connection.

"What's the cool cat right about now?" Penny asked. "and, speaking of Blackjack...how can you still hear him when you've lost your powers? Is it that Zoolingualism thing-a-thing you can do?" Penny asked, pushing away the book she'd been studying and reaching for Blackjack. She grabbed him just as he was about to escape and petted him with her usual forcefulness until he succumbed to her aggressive love and purred.

"He said we need a break, and it's not about *me* being able to hear *him*. It's *his* choice of who's able to hear him."

Penny stopped petting Blackjack mid-stroke. "He can *choose* who hears him?" She looked down at Blackjack, pouting. "Why don't you choose *me,* boy? Aunty Penny loooovvvves youuuuu." The aggressive petting ensued.

Blackjack peered up at Penny, pushing his thoughts out to her. "*Because you're an annoying, aggravating, aggressive fireball of a human. I refuse to communicate with your kind.*"

Penny practically jumped from her chair. "Oh. My. Goddess. He *talked!* Blackjack talked to me! Oh, happy day, I can hear him speak!" Penny scooped Blackjack off her lap and hugged him around his neck. A loud fart from Blackjack's back end blasted Penny before he mewed, scratched her, and took off. "Ouch! Jeez, Blackjack. Aggressive much?" Penny asked after him, rubbing the scratch mark on her hand.

"*Tell the fireball she's off my friend's list.*" Blackjack pushed the thought to Alex from down the hall.

I laughed at Penny's pout. "He says 'friends off'. Anyway, he's right. We need a time-out. Alright, ladies," I said, addressing my small but formidable team of two. "Let's take a break for now. We can reconvene in an hour."

"Sounds good to me." Penny stretched her arms above her head and yawned. "I could use some fresh air. And a hefty dose of Cheetos."

"Me too," Teddy chimed in, stifling a yawn of her own. "I'll check on the hellhounds and ensure they haven't torn up the garden again. Now that the veggies are gone and the soil turned under, it's just a big, empty mud pit. Too tempting for those two kooks."

"Takes a kook to know a kook, Ted. I'll come too. Maybe throw a frisbee for the fellows. Or maybe one of the staff.

The hounds love a good game of fetch." Penny laughed a goofy, malicious laugh.

"Thanks, ladies," I replied, grateful for their help. "I'm going to grab a quick coffee. Does anyone else care for one?"

"No, thanks, Alex. If I have caffeine this late in the day, I'll keep Cathy up all night—and not in a good way." Penny wiggled her eyebrows.

Teddy laughed. "I'll stick to the new tea I concocted earlier today. It's super yummy for my tummy, but thanks Alex." The ladies, one a witch whose powers were stripped and one a burgeoning student of mine, slipped out of the library and galloped through the castle halls to the front door. The grown women played games of hide-and-seek, dressed up in suits of armor, and regularly jumped on all the beds.

Having a bestie who owned her own freakin' castle was cool.

"Would you like me to accompany you to the kitchen?" Blackjack asked, coming out of his hiding place behind a large plant. His snarky tone was no longer clear, even through our telepathic connection, and I wondered if he was feeling okay.

"Sure, why not?" I replied with a smile, knowing he would follow me regardless of my answer.

"Excellent," he purred as we walked down the wide hallway. *"Perhaps her excellence would be so kind as to toss me a tasty treat?"*

I stifled a giggle. Ah. Food. That explained his motivation for being so sweet. "Haven't had your fill of mice, Blackjack?"

"Meh. I'm watching my figure. Mickey Mouse was hitting the waistline pretty hard. I could afford to take a break."

"So, tired of the chase, eh?" I giggled. Blackjack just

sniffed and walked ahead of me. "Ok, boy, you win. One tasty treat coming up!"

The castle kitchen was warm and inviting, with a large hearth, copper pots hanging from hooks, and aged wooden countertops worn smooth by generations of Earl Dagon's staff, Witch Hunters, and later, Museum Curators. As I moved around the room, I couldn't help but think of Blake and what he would think of me living in the castle. I was sure he would be super stoked at the idea since he wanted me to embrace my Dagon powers the last time we talked— more like fought.

Oh, the irony.

The faint scent of lavender and mint wafted through the air—remnants of Teddy's latest concoction—cooked up in the large cauldron hanging over the fire. It reminded me of Blake's shampoo. I closed my eyes and took a deep breath.

"Woman," came Blackjack's voice, jolting me back to the present. *"Your macchiato awaits."* Blackjack nodded toward Malcolm, who had anticipated my need for another shot of caffeine and saved me the painstaking task of creating it.

"Thanks, Malcolm," I murmured, taking the cup, admiring the perfectly placed steamed milk and drizzle of caramel sauce. The rich aroma of the coffee filled my senses, grounding me in the here and now.

"Your Grace. Please let me know if I can be of further assistance." Malcolm gave a slight bow before exiting the kitchen. I watched after the tall, brooding man-creature until he was out of earshot.

"Everyone has been so helpful, Blackjack. But we're no closer to finding a spell to return my and Penny's powers."

"I assume you are including Mr. Creepy in your reference to 'everyone'?"

I nodded. "Malcolm is strange, but he makes a mean macchiato." I sipped the frothy cup of goodness.

"Sure, whatever you say, your Grace," Blackjack chided as I sipped my drink. *"But you are correct in believing you're not alone in this fight. We're all here for you."*

Blackjack had been abnormally kind since my powers had been stripped, and I'd embraced my new title. Although he hadn't completely lost his snarky edge, he had dialed it down considerably. He often *willingly* comforted me, as an excellent familiar should. I assumed his recent gentleness was because he knew just how hard living in the castle and accepting the responsibility of my new title was.

His words warmed my heart, and I knew he was right. Although I missed my home on Ocean View Drive—the antique furnishings covered with large sheets, the windows papered over, and the doors locked until further notice—with my friends by my side, there was nothing we couldn't overcome.

For now, though, I would enjoy this moment of respite, savoring the sweet taste of caramel as it ebbed the weight of responsibility before diving headfirst again into the treacherous waters of witchcraft, danger, and secrecy.

Every day, the possibility of reclaiming my powers grew increasingly distant. My only hope was The Book. I didn't know if it was the key to unlocking my full potential, but it was all I had.

Day after day and night after night, I pored over its pages and the pages of books that would hopefully shed light on the secret language, my frustration mounting as I struggled to decipher its secrets.

Determined and fiercely loyal to those I loved, I refused to relinquish my quest to reclaim my powers. I knew that without them, I couldn't protect my people and—not just rule, but destroy—the Witch Hunters who sought to destroy us.

But that responsibility was taking its toll on me, as the dark circles surrounding my eyes would reveal.

Hours later, after Penny went home to Cathy and Teddy and the hounds retired to their room for the evening, I sat in the dimly lit library alone, Blackjack snuggled on the chair beside me. My fingers traced the ancient script on the yellowed pages of The Book.

This is useless.

I closed the book, got up, and stretched, walking to the large, curved library window and peering into the night sky.

I thought about my mother, locked in the Lexington County Sanatorium, catatonic under a demon's curse. The last visit resulted in Mom 'coming to' momentarily—thanks to a potion Teddy concocted—enough time for her to *see* me and tell me that "all the answers were in The Book."

I sighed heavily.

I couldn't help but feel her sense of urgency in those moments of clarity, knowing that the key to reclaiming my stolen powers was locked within those mysterious pages. And, without my powers, I couldn't bring her back from her catatonic state to ask her more about it. Even if she *could* interpret its pages, I couldn't keep her lucid long enough to do so.

My heart, mind, and soul churned like the winter wind outside, spinning and pushing against the window glass.

I returned to the desk, sat, and opened The Book, preparing for another long night of wasted time and unanswered questions.

CHAPTER
FOUR

BLAKE

I awoke with a start. Dad hovered over my single bed in one of the farmhouse bedrooms. The handmade quilt—one of many Magma and my mother had made—askew across my body. Sweat-soaked sheets cooled my skin instantly.

I had been dreaming of Alex.

My hand instinctively went to my groin, hopeful I hadn't popped a tent.

I had, but. it was more of a pup size rather than the eight-person variety.

"Dad? What's the matter? What's going on?"

"Son, get dressed. We have news." Dad, stone-faced, slipped out of the room, his heavy footfalls indicating he'd gone downstairs.

I quickly jumped in the shower, scrubbing the sweat from my skin and thoughts of Alexandra from my mind. Something was up, and I didn't need any witchy or other powers to tell me it wasn't great. I dried, dressed, and was downstairs in the warm kitchen within minutes of Dad rousing me. Magma, Mom, and Dad were around the table. A hot cup of coffee—black, the way the Goddess—I mean God, no, Goddess, intended, was waiting for me at the table.

I sat, took a sip of the hot liquid, and peered over my cup as three pairs of eyes stared back at me.

"Okay, what's up? And judging from your faces, I assume it's not good."

"That depends, Son," Dad said.

"On what?"

"On point of view."

I blew out a harsh breath and ran a hand through my hair. "*Dad*. Speak. Please. It's way too early for guessing games."

Mom reached for Dad's hand across the table. Since I hadn't been near my parents for twenty years, I wasn't accustomed to their silent language, so I couldn't tell if that meant for him to go on or to stay quiet.

It meant go on, apparently.

Dad took a deep breath. "We have news from the underground."

I perked up mid-sip.

"Your Alexandra is alive."

I coughed, choking on the hot liquid. Covering my mouth, I coughed some more.

Alex was alive.

It took every ounce of energy to stay in my seat. I wanted to jump up, clap my hands, fist pump the air, and run to her side. However, looking at the three faces across the table from me dimmed my excitement. "That's amazing news—isn't it?" I asked. "To me, at least. But you three look like you just lost your kittens. What's going on?"

Mom spoke up. "According to our underground sources, she had her powers stripped and was about to be burned on the pyre alongside another witch, Penny, I believe, when..." she paused.

"When what?" I released my grip on my coffee mug before crushing it.

Dad continued. "When Earl Dagon appeared and named her Dagon Queen."

My body flushed a heated sweat, and not from the hot liquid.

"*Queen?*" I squeaked. "What does *that* mean?"

Magma spoke softly. "She's now Queen of the Witch Hunters, Blake."

I stared, mouth agape, at the three of them. Everything from the blink of my Mother's beautiful eyes to the late autumn fly buzzing around the room was in super-slow motion. I bobble-headed from one face to another and back again.

Then, sucking in a huge breath, I *laughed*.

Booming, boisterous laughter escaped me. Relieved, I laughed until tears leaked down my cheeks and onto the table. I wiped my face with my shirtsleeve, then slapped the table, laughing some more. The three of them jumped, staring at me wide-eyed.

"You've *got* to be kidding me!" I sputtered, clutching my sides.

"I wish we were, Son. But it's true. It even made the front page of the news." Dad produced his iPad and slid it across to me. The webpage was on the Castle Point Daily News. I stared at a grainy, black-and-white photo of Alex, *my Alex*. I recognized it as one from her Apothecary and Therapy websites. The caption under the picture read, "*Former witch and practicing therapist, Alexandra Heale, has been named Queen of the Order of Witch Hunters by the late Earl Dagon himself."*

Well, suck me dry and call me dusty.

It was true.

Alexandra was the queen. And only a few days after I'd asked her—no, begged her—to embrace her Dagon powers, arguing that she could *rule.* And now, here she was, doing exactly that. I wanted to embrace the paper, my closest thing to Alexandra.

A nagging piece of truth itched like a mosquito bite on a hot day but was more...humorous.

I was a witch.

Alexandra's witch powers had been stripped.

Alexandra was the Queen of the Witch Hunters.

Oh, the irony.

I couldn't help but grin. Alexandra just *had* to see the irony in this herself. My mind locked on a mental image of Alexandra, and I wondered how she was handling it all. I wished I could be there to help her.

She was *in charge.* Which meant she could *command* the hunters to do...what exactly?

"That's what we hoped you could tell us, Son." My Dad interjected.

"Dad, stop reading my thoughts."

"Sorry, Son, but we need to know. Do you think Alexandra, now that she's queen, could be an ally to the witches... or an enemy?" The look of concern on my father's face made me stop and think. *Could* Alexandra embrace her new title and be a threat to the underground witch population? She had to know where most witches were operating—at least locally. The hunters would have a heyday if Alexandra gave them directions to the witch's locations.

But no, she would never go against her kind. The

thought was ludicrous. I shook my head, staring at my coffee mug as Magma poured me a fresh cup, topping it off with a hefty dollop of bourbon.

I shook my head. "Alexandra would never endanger the witch population. If anything, her being crowned is a good thing. Was there any other news?" I skimmed through the article, but the details were brief. It had only happened a couple of nights ago on Samhain, so likely, there wasn't much else to report.

"I hope you're right, Son. And if you are, do you think she could help us? Right now, she's the furthest inside the Witch Hunter's world than any of us have ever thought possible. It gives us hope—if she's kept her loyalty to the witch population."

I nodded slowly, my thoughts churning in time with my stomach. Magma must have heard my stomach growl and, thinking it meant hunger, took to the stove to finish preparing breakfast. "I'm right. I know Alex. She's loyal to a fault. She's our ally."

Even saying so, I forced a seed of disbelief from my mind.

If Alex's loyalty had shifted, then the shit show was about to explode to epic proportions.

"Dad, what about Jeff Delbert? He took Penny for himself...was he...successful at stripping her of her powers?" My throat went dry. I could barely *think* of the right words to use. Power stripping hadn't happened in over a half-century. It wasn't like going to the local coffee shop and ordering a frothy concoction from a witch-hating barista.

"According to the article, yes. He was."

"And, Alexandra? Who stripped her of her powers?"

The coffee reference made me think of Alex, wondering again if she was okay.

"Earl Dagon took those for himself. Well, not for *himself*, but...he just...took them."

I nodded solemnly as my brain groaned under the weight of processing the information. My stomach formed a tight knot.

It was all my fault.

If I hadn't spoken up at the Witch Hunter gathering about Penny...if I'd just stayed silent, none of this would have happened.

My shoulders shook off the thought as a chill rippled up my spine.

At least Alex was alive. The rest we could deal with.

"Dad, what about Gordon Roberts? He would have been in charge of the ceremony. Any news on him?"

Dad nodded, chuckling. "No doubt he was upset about the whole affair, but my sources say he swore allegiance to the new queen. That's something, I guess."

Magma placed a plate of food before me, and I dug in, talking with a mouthful. "Which technically means he's on our side. He's not your source?"

"No, he's never been a source, Son. Why do you ask?"

"Just...curious. I'm not convinced he had anything to do with the death threats that led to your fake deaths. If he is Alexandra's ally, then...well, I suppose he's staying true to Earl Dagon's law."

No biggie. Just that the man who practically raised me, hired me out of cadet training, and enlisted me into the Order may be the one who intended to leave me parentless.

Dad's eyes rolled to the ceiling, and he sighed resignedly. "We can't trust anyone, Blake. Not Gordon, not

Jeffrey, and...not even your Alexandra. Not until we can be sure she's still a witch. In her heart, at least."

I murmured an agreement before finishing my breakfast, tossing my stupid thoughts aside. I just knew Alexandra would be loathe in her new role. She had to be. And, if she were, she would do anything to get her powers back.

A renewed excitement and determination spurned me on. I wanted my witch powers unbound, to learn my craft, and to get back to Alexandra as soon as possible.

"Can we speed up this un-binding ceremony thing? Like, say, now?" I asked my parents, who stopped mid-bite to stare at me.

Magma chuckled and continued to down her breakfast.

"Uh, Son. We usually do the unbinding at midnight, under the moon..." Mom injected.

"Sure, sure. But it *can* be done anytime, no?"

"What's the rush, Son?" Dad asked.

I raked my hands through my hair and took a deep breath. My impatience was getting the better of me. "The sooner I can harness my powers, the sooner I can get back to Alex and help her take down the hunters."

Dad nodded, looked at Mom, then Magma, and smiled back at me. "Ok, Son. We'll start after breakfast."

I couldn't help it. I pumped my fist high in the air.

FIVE

ALEXANDRA

T he scent of blackberry wine wafted from the goblet as I swirled it, the deep purple liquid catching the candlelight. Penny's eyes were excitedly bright across the ornate twenty-foot heavy oak dining table. We had moved most of our research material and books from the library to the formal dining room to spread out farther than we could on the smaller, although equally grand, library desk. A fire crackled in the massive fireplace near the table, warming the room. A layer of sweaters kept the remaining chill at bay.

"Hey, Alex, I forgot to ask. Did you hear about the murder in Castle Point?" Penny's voice echoed in the massive chamber as she yelled from the opposite end of the table. "Someone was beheaded, and the head's missing!"

I shuddered, images of a bloodied neck stump flashing through my mind. "That's grisly," I muttered.

"What did you say?" Penny yelled.

"I said that's grisly," I yelled back.

"Oh, yeah, it is. Totes gross, if you ask me." Penny yelled.

"I agree," I said.

"What?" Penny yelled, encircling her hand around her ear so she could hear me better.

"I said...never mind. For Goddess' sake, Penny, would you just come closer?" I yelled, gesturing for her to come my way and laughing.

Penny got up from her seat. "Be there in about five or ten minutes, your Highness!" she yelled, exaggerating a slow-motion run to my end of the table.

When she finally arrived, my cheeks were sore from laughing so hard. Thank the Goddess for Penny's comedy. Despite losing her powers to Jeffrey Deibert, she kept the dark thoughts from surfacing. She came to the castle almost every day when she could pull herself away from her job as a nurse and her wife, Cathy, to help me find the spell to replenish our powers.

Not that she was concerned with losing her powers, to begin with.

Now, she was on even ground with her wife and staff of nurses at the hospital; she didn't have to hide in plain sight anymore. However, she understood we might fight against the disgruntled Witch Hunter population, which meant all hands—and witchy powers—on deck.

"Pen, what about the murder? And why are you telling me this?" The urgency of spell-finding made me impatient for stories or shenanigans—an unfortunate side-effect of losing my powers and becoming a queen.

Penny's smile faded. "It's my cousin, Carrigan. She owns the Critt Family Memorial Funeral Home and Gardens. She says she saw the ghost of the headless man clear as day. Claims the whole thing seems fishy."

"Carrigan saw a ghost?" I stared at her in surprise. Not that I should be surprised. Anyone could if they were open to it or the spirit insisted on being seen. It could happen to anyone, even me. Which was good, or I couldn't communicate with Cressy, which would kill me.

Penny nodded, her brow furrowed with concern. "This is the first time since her father left her the family Corpse Collector business. She doesn't know what to make of it. It's freaked her out. She wants to meet with you."

I stared at Pen, wide-eyed. "Corpse Collector?"

"Yeah, you know, because she works with corpses as Castle Point's Coroner, Funeral Director, Cemetery Superintendent, and Historian. Duh." Penny rolled her eyes. "I also call her the Crazy Crochet Cat Lady. Because, you know, she crochets and has cats...and...stuff."

I chuckled. "Interesting title. But I guess the community owes her a thanks. I wouldn't want any of those jobs, and one cat is more than enough for me." I grinned at Blackjack, who was lounging on the massive table, soaking up a ray of winter sun cast across the table.

"Yeah, me neither. I've seen my share of dead bodies at the hospital, but she's the one people call when bodies have been *found*. Sometimes, *days* after they've died..."

"Ew!" Teddy burst in, hearing the latter part of the conversation. "That's super icky."

I nodded my agreement. "They wouldn't be in the best condition in that case."

"Nope. And super-ripe. I mean, phew! Super stink-a-thon." Penny wafted a hand in front of her face. "Like, not just Rigor mortis, but...ew, I can't even..."

"Yes, please don't. We get the picture. Why does she want to meet with me?"

"So you can...you know...do your hypnosis stuff and

maybe help her figure out why she's now seeing ghosts after years in the biz. And this ghost, in particular."

I considered Penny's request. I had closed my therapy practice right after becoming queen and moving into the castle. My priorities were finding the spell to give me my powers back. My clients understood, not that they had much choice, and they all seemed to respect my new role as queen. None of my clients were Witch Hunters. "I'm not taking any new clients, Penny. Not any clients, period. You know that."

"But she needs your help, Alex. She's terrified." Penny pleaded.

I hesitated. Getting involved with a murder investigation wasn't on my to-do list. But if Carrigan had developed some psychic ability, or, better yet, witchy abilities that were finally arising, she'd need guidance from an experienced witch.

Even one who had lost her powers.

Even from me.

"Alright," I sighed. "I'll talk to her. But I can't make any promises beyond that. Not until I know more."

Penny's shoulders sagged in relief. "Thank you, Alex. I knew I could count on you."

I managed a faint smile in return. But inside, my thoughts churned like the gathering storm clouds outside. A headless ghost, a gruesome murder, and possibly a new witch in our midst?

Something wicked was brewing in Castle Point. And it seemed I was fated to be at the center of it. I wished Blake were around to help me. Despite our differences, we had become a good team.

I pushed thoughts of Blake aside when Malcolm entered the dining room.

"Dinner is served, your Grace. At the kitchen table, as requested."

"Thank you, Malcolm. We'll be there in an instant." Malcolm bowed his head slightly and retreated from the room.

Teddy gave a little shudder. "I can't quite get used to having 'Lurch' as a butler. He gives me the heebie geebies."

"Shh, Teddy. He might hear you." I scolded, smiling. She had a point. He was a little creepy. I peered out of the dining area into the dark hall, expecting to see Malcolm's back as he walked away. He was gone.

"Maybe he's not a man, but someone's science experiment." Penny guffawed, stretching her arms out in front of her, zombie-like, and walking toward Teddy, sending her into a fit of giggles.

I rolled my eyes. "Okay, you two. Let's take a break for dinner, then go talk to Carrigan."

Penny whooped.

"Can I come too? To Carrigan's, I mean." Teddy asked.

"By all means. The more, the merrier."

She and Penny did a fancy hand-slapping handshake, one they've been working on but never entirely perfected. I broke through the slap-happy duo, smiling at my two goofy gal pals as we made our way to the castle kitchen and the delicious spread the chef had prepared.

CHAPTER
SIX

BLAKE

The pungent scent of incense overwhelmed me as I entered the candlelit backyard. Mom, Dad, and Magma were seated around a large circle they had laid out, bordered by candles and adorned with white, arcane symbols scrawled with what looked like salt. An altar stood near one side of the circle. They got up to greet me. This was it - the moment my powers would be unbound.

I was born a witch and about to reclaim my birthright.

I still couldn't believe it.

I was about to have powers, and Alexandra just lost hers.

The weirdness of it all and the irony weren't lost on me, but there was a lot to learn before I could be of any use.

I pictured Alex's face, remembering her strength and bravery when she used her powers to save—among others—me. If she could harness and control those powers, then maybe...just maybe I could, too.

I glanced from one parent to the other, meeting their expectant gazes, and nodded. "I'm ready."

Dad's eyes crinkled with relief and pride. He squeezed my shoulder. "Then let us begin."

Magma beckoned me forward. "It is time, young witch. Step into the circle."

My pulse quickened as I moved into the center of the candle-lit circle. Despite the chilly air, I could feel hot energy swirling around me, calling to the dormant magic within.

Mom lifted her trembling hands high into the air, murmuring words in a language I didn't understand. Dad and Magma joined in. A surreal feeling swept through me with every word they uttered. Before my eyes, a soft glow began emanating from their palms, casting an eerie, flickering light across the yard. I gasped, my pulse pounding in my ears.

It was real.

Magic was real.

And it was about to be mine.

I had seen Alexandra wield the same kind of power, and I had been gobsmacked when she did, but seeing it happen and being unable to do it was one thing.

This was quite another.

Mom, Dad, and Magma held hands, forming a circle around me. The candle flames leaped higher, fueled by their power. A soft wind stirred, whipping my hair as the chanting reached a crescendo until they broke apart.

I trembled as Magma slipped an ornate dagger from a sheath below her cloak. She grasped my hand, turning my palm upward. She met my eyes, then cut into my palm. I hissed but did not pull away. She carried the bloodied dagger to the altar and allowed three drops of blood to fall into what looked like a brass incense burner. The same kind I had seen Father Donovan use during church services. Magma used the dagger to mix my blood with a few pinches of some herbs and other....I didn't know what.

Magma carefully grasped the chain of the burner and brought it over to me, holding it near my face. Tendrils of stinky smoke curled around my face and eyes. I held my breath. Wincing, I attempted to keep my head from turning away from the disgusting mixture. I was grateful she hadn't concocted the mix into a drink. That would staunch my desire to unbind my powers.

She ran the burner up and down my body, side to side, back to front, chanting a strange language all the while. When she was done, she placed the burner back on the altar, raised her hands to the air, and chanted;

"By blood, we unbind. By craft we free." Magma's voice rang out. *"Blake Sheraton, reclaim your destiny."*

A millisecond of expectation passed before a shockwave rippled through me. Suddenly, I floated, surrounded by stars and purple light, but my feet never left the ground. My heart beat faster, and I could feel...something...power, perhaps, coursing through my veins. A brilliant flash of light exploded through me. My whole body tingled, magic surging like a tidal wave. I rode the wave up, down, up, down, not in control of my body.

I cried out, overwhelmed by the raw energy now unleashed. Magma, Mom, and Dad joined hands again, chanting louder and faster as the energy waves flowed through me. The ceremony was a blur of archaic words and aromatic herbs, the energy spiking heat in every pore of my body as though tiny quills were piercing me, inside and out.

I trembled as the bindings fell away, magic thrumming through my veins. By the time it ended, I was utterly exhausted. I opened my eyes and looked at the three witches smiling down at me. During the ceremony, I had fallen to my knees. I took a few deep breaths, steadying my nerves before awkwardly standing. Dad held my arm and supported my back as I wavered, threatening to fall to the ground again.

I looked around, beyond the sacred circle, into the woods, and up to the waxing moon. The world seemed brighter somehow, full of promise and potential. Then it ebbed, settling into my core with a contented hum. I gazed at my hands in awe. Sparks danced across my fingertips.

I was reborn.

"His powers have awakened," Magma intoned.

Mom and Dad enveloped me in a tight hug, Mom's flowery perfume and Dad's musky aftershave filling my senses. "Welcome to our world, Son."

I returned their embrace, overwhelmed with emotion. For so long, I'd felt lost, adrift, missing my parents, but now everything made sense.

This was where I belonged.

I rested on the porch swing, a steeping hot cup of Magma's tea in my hand. I lifted a hand in front of my face, then slowly pointed a finger toward a garden gnome Magma had sitting on the porch railing. A tingling in the tip of my finger pronounced a tiny spark of white light that burst forward to the gnome, popping it off the porch to the bushes below.

Shit. I hope it didn't break.

I was about to get up and check, but my wobbly legs refused to cooperate, so I sat back just as Dad stepped out of the house to join me. I quickly hid my hand and my grin. I wasn't supposed to start 'playing' with my powers until Magma, Mom, and Dad were ready for me.

This was going to be fun.

Dad's face told a different story. The smile lines that gently creased his eyes were replaced with worry.

"Dad, what's wrong?"

"More news from the underground, Blake. And it's not good."

I sat slightly taller in the swing and placed my tea on the table. Fear gripped my heart. "Is it Alex? Did something happen to her?"

Dad shook his head. I relaxed a little. "No, Son. Well, maybe. We don't know. The Witch Hunters have been revolting against Alex's reign. We fear they will increase their hunt for witches despite having a new queen."

I brushed a hand through my hair.

Dammit. Despite having new powers, I still felt... powerless.

"Can anyone tell us if Alexandra is okay?"

Dad nodded. "I'll ask. What we know for sure is the Witch Hunters are planning a conclave. They're planning to take down the queen, Son. We assume she doesn't know." He stood up. I stood with him, looking him in the eyes.

He clasped my shoulder. "This is a lot to take in, but we have little time. The conclave is in a few weeks, and we must be ready."

I nodded, determination steeling my spine. I would do whatever it took to stop them, to make Alex and my parents proud. I pictured her raven hair flying in the wind, those piercing green eyes flashing defiantly.

She would never go down without a fight.

And neither would I.

A thought occurred to me. "Dad, is Gordon leading the conclave?"

Dad glanced at his shoes, absently rubbing a spot on

the porch floor with his toes. "Well, I'll put it this way. When I was High Commander, only one person would have the right to call the conclave in the first place...me."

I nodded. A knot formed in the pit of my belly. "So, do you think Gordon has sided with the hunters?"

"Not necessarily. I think it is more likely that he wants to exercise some control over his troops. He probably called the conclave to talk some sense into all of them. Remind them of Earl Dagon's command."

"I hope you're right. Do you think Jeff Deibert will be there? After he swooped in and kidnapped Penny, I don't trust the guy."

"Jeff is high in the Order, so I assume he must be. Along with as many other conclave hunters worldwide."

"Where do you think they'll hold the conclave? Castle Dagon?" *It would be good to know where they set the meeting so we can plan a tactical assault.*

"I suppose so? And you're right. We need to find out to plan accordingly." I raised an eyebrow at Dad. I was still getting used to his ability to read my thoughts. He ignored me and continued, "I guess that would depend on whether the new queen would even allow it."

Right...the new queen. Alexandra. Another thing that would take getting used to. Using Alex's name and queen in the same sentence. "What do you think will happen, Dad? What would the Witch Hunters do if Alexandra finds out about the conclave and stops it?"

Dad swallowed hard. "War, Son. We'd have a war..."

Beads of sweat tangled in my hair despite the winter wind chilling the rest of me. Alex was alive, but her chances of survival against the hunters weren't great. She needed... me. I steeled my body against the chill. "Then we have work to do." I stood tall, forcing my legs to cooperate as magic hummed through me.

If the Hunters wanted a war, they'd have one.

Dad squeezed my hand, pride shining in her eyes. "That's my boy. Now, let's start your lessons."

I followed him to the backyard, which Magma and Mom had transformed from a large, sacred circle to an obstacle course of various objects and structures. I briefly wondered how they had cleaned up and reset the yard to its current state, then scolded myself.

Of course. Magic.

And this was my new playground.

The full moon seemed to pulse, bathing the late fall ground in silver light. Magma stood waiting, her wizened face etched with excitement.

My palms grew clammy.

"For years, we've worked secretly to take down the Witch Hunters from within," Dad said. "But now, it's time for our powers to be free, and we finish what we started— as a family."

He turned to me, his eyes blazing with conviction. "It's time for your powers to be free, Son."

This was the family legacy they had hinted at but never revealed.

I was the son of witches.

As fear and wonder battled inside me, I knew my life would never be the same.

Dad gave me an encouraging smile. "I know this is a lot to take in. But we're here for you. Today has been the start of an incredible journey."

I glanced between the three of them. "What kind of powers will I have?" My mind swirled with images of flying broomsticks and bubbling cauldrons.

Mom let out a small laugh. "Patience, my son. We will find out together. All in due time. "

I stood tall, ready to get to work to take my place at their side.

The Hunters did not know who they were messing with now.

My family would show them the true meaning of power.

CHAPTER
SEVEN

ALEXANDRA

The pungent stench of formaldehyde wafted through the air like a perfume by Dracula's chemist. I tiptoed past the small, dimly lit morgue, feeling like I'd entered a B-movie horror set. Penny led us down the hall to Carrigan's office. I took a deep breath to steel my nerves as Penny knocked on the door.

This wasn't exactly how I'd planned to spend my evening. Who expects a friendly chat with a Corpse Collector? But Penny was like family to me, and when family needed help, you didn't say, "Sorry, can't make it. I have a date with a dusty old book that nobody can interpret, that may or may not hold the secret spell I'm desperate to find."

Not the time to be selfish, Alex.

Carrigan, mascara smudged under her bloodshot eyes, flung the door open like she'd seen a ghost, which she recently had. Plus, working in the morgue, it was more than likely the first sighting wouldn't be her last. Her hands shook like she was playing a never-ending game of jazz hands.

Penny leaped forward, wrapping Carrigan in a tight hug. "Hey, it's okay, the Ghostbusters are here." Carrigan feigned a smile but looked exhausted, sporting purple bags under her eyes that even designer shades couldn't hide. The past few days had been a thriller, and not in the fun MJ way.

As Teddy, Penny, and I stepped inside the office, we walked into the feline version of Grand Central Station. Cats of all shapes and sizes lounged like they owned the place. Carrigan was in the middle of a high-stakes cat-removal operation.

"I apologize for the number of cats. As a foster mom for the local rescue, I have a hard time turning away any of these adorable creatures." Carrigan unwrapped a fresh lint roller and ran it over the couch and chairs.

I grinned. If lint rollers were currency, she'd be a millionaire by now. "I have a cat. I know how you feel. These are all rescues? None of them are yours?" Teddy and Penny oohed and awed over the frisky felines, scooping up the cooperative ones for snuggles.

"Oh, no. I haven't adopted...yet. Although I am pretty fond of this fellow." Carrigan scooped up a brown and red mottled mixed breed with dark black brows and a thin black line above his upper lip that mimicked a pencil-thin mustache that reminded me of Cressy. "I named him 'Alastair' because he looks so aristocratic."

"I have to agree." I stroked his regal head. "He's adorable and reminds me of someone I know who's also very...' aristocratic.' So...Penny filled me in on a few things," I began, eyeing the fluffy white cat who seemed intent on claiming my freshly lint-rolled seat. I mean, who could blame her? Cats had a sixth sense of finding the comfiest spot in the room. I hurried over, and she reluctantly shared the small couch, giving me a look. "She said you saw a headless ghost?"

Carrigan nodded, her gaze distant, like she was revisiting the scene. "Thank you for coming. I didn't know what to do," she said, her voice wobbled.

I reached over and gave her arm an encouraging pat, which was about as comforting as a cold, clammy handshake from a ghost. I checked myself.

Have some patience, Alex. She's scared, for Goddess's sake.

"Hey, it's okay. Take a few deep breaths." I softened my tone and patted her hand again. Her skin was cool to the touch, probably because her office and morgue were in the cold basement of the funeral home.

Penny gave the couch a suspicious look as if it might turn into a cat at any moment before collapsing onto the couch beside me. Teddy quickly squeezed into the remaining space on the other side of me. Carrigan busied herself with making tea, which seemed a solid choice in this chilly situation. The sound of pouring water and the faint hiss of the kettle brought a touch of normalcy to this paranormal party.

"So, Carrigan," I said, sipping my chamomile tea. "What exactly happened?"

With seriousness, she began, "One minute, I was prepping Mr. McCafferty's body - not the headless man - for his viewing, and the next, this creepy thing appeared right next to me. Scared me half to death."

"That's super scary," Teddy chimed in, her voice tinged with that mix of fascination and horror you get when watching a particularly gruesome, true crime documentary.

"Also, I didn't know Mr. McCafferty crossed over! So sad. I wonder who will inherit his '57 Chevy Bel Air…"

I shot Teddy a look. She got the message and fell silent, sipping her tea. Carrigan wiped away a few tears, and I couldn't help but wonder if they were cat allergy-induced.

"And you've never seen a ghost before, right?" I asked, raising an eyebrow and ignoring the cat snuggling up to my leg.

Carrigan nodded vigorously, her short, dark hair bouncing. "Right. This is the first time."

I considered this momentarily, taking in the subtle aroma of chamomile tea mixed with the faint scent of cat fur. "Carrigan, if you don't mind me asking, how old are you?"

Carrigan shrugged. "I don't mind. I turned forty last month. Why?"

"That checks," I mused, taking another sip of tea. "Sometimes, when someone…" I hesitated, searching for a word, "*Special* is coming into abilities they've never had; it's at or around your age."

"*Abilities?* You think this seeing-ghosts thing is an ability?" Carrigan looked horrified like she'd just seen a ghost. I peeked around the room and then gave my head a shake.

"Not necessarily. It could be as simple as this ghost insisted on being seen."

"But why me?"

"That, I cannot answer. Sorry."

Carrigan gave a slight shrug, my tea cup offering its silent support. "Well, it's only happened once so far, so perhaps this is a special case…"

"Does the Sheriff's department have any leads? On the murder?" Penny asked, her voice tinged with curiosity because who wouldn't be curious about headless corpses and ghostly apparitions?

Carrigan shook her head. "They rarely include me in their investigations. We don't have a lot of murders in Castle Point, thank goodness. Regardless, my part of the picture is only the coroner's business and body removal after the deputies finished their investigation."

"Yeah, likely you won't get any answers from the department. Besides, ghosts are not their realm," I said, sipping my tea. "You have only seen it one time? Anything else weird happened then or since?"

Carrigan nodded her head vigorously, like a bobblehead caught in a windstorm. It took every ounce of energy for me not to reach out and grab her head in my hands.

"Yes! The corpse spoke to me! Or, more like *through* me. I can't even explain it, but it scared the hell out of me."

My interest was piqued, and I leaned forward. "What did the apparition say?"

Carrigan took a shattered breath, her trembling hands adding a percussive element to her story. "I don't know. Or I don't remember...it's...fuzzy."

Penny coned her fingers to her hand and shouted. "Sounds like a job for Super Therapist Alexandra Heale! Da da da da!"

I hoped Carrigan didn't pick up on my major eye-roll.

"I have to admit, I also think I need therapy..." Carrigan agreed with her cousin.

I nodded. "There *is* something we can do to find out what the ghost said. Have you ever been under hypnosis?"

Carrigan shook her head. "No, but if you think it would help, I'm up for anything."

Penny pumped a fist in the air. "Yesss! Let's do it."

"Okay. Um..." I looked around the sparse office. "Here?"

There was a metal desk, a couple of chairs, and a small cat-hair-laden couch. Not even a plant. Not that one could live down in this cold dungeon. The only other offering was a wall of certificates announcing Carrigan's many professional hats.

"Sure." Carrigan nodded. "Good a place as any. What do I need to do?"

"Well, would you be more comfortable lying on the couch? Or is the chair okay?"

Carrigan pushed her chair away from the desk. "I think I'm good here. What next?" An excitable child replaced the previously depressed, anxious woman.

"Okay, just sit back, relax, and close your eyes." When she had done so, I started the relaxation suggestions. "Take a deep, cleansing breath. Good. Fill your lungs to the top and release slowly, feeling your muscles relax. Good."

I had Carrigan take a few more breaths, asking her to focus on relaxing all body parts sequentially. I could feel Penny and Teddy relaxing, flanking me on either side of the couch. A slight elbow jab to each of them brought them out of it.

"Okay, Carrigan, I'm going to count from five down to one, and when I reach one, you will be deeply relaxed and ready to remember." I counted her down.

In no time at all, Carrigan's head began rolling forward. I knew she was deep enough to question. "Carrigan, can you imagine when the headless ghost visited you? Let me know when you have that in your mind."

Carrigan nodded. "Okay. I see him."

"Good. Now, he spoke to you. Can you focus on what he said?"

Her head rolled from side to side as if straining to listen.

"It…he…said, '*Murder has risen, and Murder shall reign, and Murder shall take another again. You have been warned.*'"

Penny, Teddy, and I exchanged puzzled glances. "What the heckin' heck does that mean?" Teddy whispered, her voice a mix of confusion and amusement.

"I do not know," I admitted, taking another sip of tea and continuing the questioning. "Carrigan, did he mean that as a personal attack? A warning, just for you?"

She shook her head, her hair bouncing around again, slower this time. "I don't know if he meant it as a threat to me."

"Did it say anything else?"

Carrigan paused. "No. That was it."

"Okay, very good. You did great. I will count from one up to five, and when I reach five, you will feel refreshed and wide awake; the anxiety of seeing the ghost will be gone. One…" I counted her up.

Carrigan's eyes fluttered open, but she didn't smile.

"You okay?" I asked.

"That was cool but also scary. I don't know why I can suddenly see ghosts. But I swear if this one comes at me again…and what did he mean by '*Murder has risen, and Murder shall reign?*'"

I nodded, raking a hand through my hair, which probably now smelled like chamomile-infused cat fur. "I agree. It's pretty terrifying and confusing. The question is, what or who is 'Murder'? Did he mean the *act* of murder or someone named 'Murder'? It's not clear."

"Me thinks we have a demon on our hands." Penny wiggled her eyebrows.

I sighed again. "It's possible, Pen. The question is, what do we do about it?"

"A...a *demon?*" The color drained from Carrigan's face faster than you can say "boo."

"Yeah. Sorry, cuz, but demons are real. Ask...well...pretty much anyone." Penny went to her cousin and wrapped an arm around her shoulder. "Can you help her, Alex? Figure out a way to stop this...whatever it is?"

Helping her would take precious time away from my research. But leaving her to face this alone felt wrong. She was Penny's family, after all. "Look, I know you're scared, but getting involved puts us both in danger," I whispered. "Without my powers, I'm about as useful as a toaster in a bathtub when dealing with demons, if that's what this is."

Carrigan's face fell. She set down her tea and gripped my hands from across the coffee table, her hands clammy and cold. "Please, Alex. I don't know who else to turn to. You're the only one who might understand what's happening to me."

I bit my lip. I could help discreetly, quietly. Ask Cressy his opinion and if he can give me any answers from the other side. Then I remembered I hadn't called upon Cressy since the power-stripping ceremony where Dagon named me Queen of the Witch Hunters.

I tugged at the small vial of Cressy's ashes dangling from my earring. I'd have to get Teddy's help with summoning him again. Hopefully, he could give me some insight into what Carrigan had seen and what to do about it with my limited capabilities. Also, I couldn't risk the Witch Hunters knowing I was delving into anything related to magic. That would turn my situation from bad to worse before you could say...well...*witch*.

If things got dicey, I'd bail.

"Okay," I relented. "But we have to be careful. No one can know about this, got it?"

Relief flooded Carrigan's face. This wasn't over, not by a long shot. But at least now she had us to turn to.

This wasn't exactly how I'd envisioned spending my time, but the witch's creed still applied to me, powers or no.

Help the innocent.

Carrigan needed my help; I had to try, at least.

EIGHT

BLAKE

"Son! You're going to start a bloody forest fire. *Focus.* Try again." Dad called out as I missed my mark and hit another tree.

It had been *days* since the resurgence of my powers, and the obstacle course of targets, football tackle dummies, and tin cans Dad, Mom, and Magma set up for me in the backyard remained, unfortunately, intact.

However, scorch marks and broken branches littered the trees surrounding Magma's yard. This magic thing was taking some getting used to.

Magma pointed a garden hose toward the latest coniferous victim and sprayed, snuffing out the threat.

I ran a hand through my hair and sighed. At least I was hitting *something.* Dad cast a look of frustration my way.

Mom saw the look. "Lucas, it's only been a few days since he got his powers back," she reminded him.

"I know, Meredith, but it's a matter of some urgency. He must perfect his aim before we can ascend on the hunters."

"I'm right here, guys. And I can hear you." I waved at them both. Mom turned to me and smiled.

"Blake, just close your eyes for a minute, will you?"

I sighed heavily but did as she asked.

"Good, now, take a deep breath. Think about the power within your own hands as you breathe. *Feel* the energy coursing through your veins. This is your *power*, Blake. What you were born with, and it wants to cooperate with you. Grab hold of a *reason* to use your energy, Blake. For the highest and greatest good of all."

I breathed deeply, feeling spikes of energy flow from somewhere deep inside me and vibrating into my fingers. "I can feel...something."

"Good. Now, take another deep breath. And when you release that breath, open your eyes and push your energy toward a target, nice and easy."

I did what she asked. Letting out a breath, I focused the energy into my hands, opened my eyes, and, rather than throwing it, *pressed* it out toward the tackle dummy.

Direct hit.

Sparks and a small flame burst open, then quickly died.

"Wow! Did you see that? I did it!" As Magma, Mom, and Dad clapped and laughed, I pumped a fist into the air.

"Great job, Son. Now, think you can do that again?"

I nodded, closed my eyes, conjured my energy, and *pushed* harder this time.

Direct hit again!

The tackle dummy blew backward with the force and lit on fire. Magma quickly cranked the garden hose open and sprayed it down so Dad could rest it upright.

"Honey, that was perfect!" Mom hugged me hard. I squeezed her back, drawing in her unique scent.

My thoughts drifted to Alexandra. I missed her rose

perfume, raven hair, and those damn perfect lips. Wondering how she was getting on in her new role as queen, I could imagine all the grumbling she'd be doing, not enjoying the role but taking it on despite her hatred for Earl Dagon and all things Witch Hunter. It made sense for her to *be* in the role. As queen, she had commanded the hunters to end the hunts for witches.

Pretty ballsy. Also, dangerous.

She landed in a challenging situation, potentially disastrous if the hunters followed through with their plans and turned on her. Determination flooded through me, my protective senses settling deep into my bones. The hunter's conclave was a couple of weeks away. The pressure I had been feeling to harness and control my powers re-surged. I released Mom from the hug and turned to the task at hand.

Perfect my aim, learn my new skills, and help Alexandra, whatever the cost.

Because she meant more to me than my life.

Because I loved her.

I didn't close my eyes this time. Keeping Alexandra in the forefront of my thoughts, I launched large and small balls of energy into the arena. I hit the tackling dummy, then the bulls-eye, then the cans, one at a time, tossing them off the picnic table. I didn't miss a beat or a target. And I didn't set the surrounding forest on fire.

I stopped and looked at the trio of seasoned teachers as they stared at the objects, then at me, their mouths agape. Robust laughing, clapping, and cheering ensued.

"Amazing, Son. You're doing it. I'm so proud." Dad patted me rigorously on the back.

"Thanks, Dad. I'll keep practicing. You guys go on inside. It's getting cold out here."

Dad nodded, slipped his hand in Mom's, and turned to the house. Magma gave me a quick squeeze.

"You did good, boy. Thinking of Alexandra is the key. Keep her in your thoughts as you do your work. She's your driving point of light in a wicked world."

I nodded, still slightly startled, when one of the three read my thoughts. This is a constant reminder to keep my thoughts about Alexandra clean. "I am, and I will."

"Good. I'll make us some hot chocolate and get the grimoire ready. Spell casting 101 is coming up!"

"Sounds good, Magma. One question."

Her light blue eyes danced in the cresting light. "Yes?"

"What's a grimoire?"

Magma raised a slender, bony finger in the air, her long silver hair blowing in the breeze. A tiny spark of light zapped from her finger as she cackled—literally cackled. "Ah, dear boy. You have so much to learn. I guess the ways of the witch have so far eluded you."

I laughed. "Well, sure. I didn't have anyone to teach me this stuff, and the witchy ways aren't exactly common knowledge to a Witch Hunter, so..."

Magma nodded her head thoughtfully. "A grimoire is a record of your family's history and spell casting. It is your *legacy*. There are hundreds of pieces of knowledge tucked within its pages that you will—no, *must*—learn."

"Sounds pretty daunting. Also pretty interesting."

"You can learn who you are through its pages." Magma smiled and turned toward the house.

I watched her open the creaky screen door and slip inside to prepare a delicious chocolate concoction for the evening ahead.

The opportunity to learn who you really are.

Something they should have taught me since birth.

Something that was stolen from me and my family when my parents decided I needed to be protected and bound my powers.

The idea was understandable and frustrating and brought my thoughts to the Witch Hunters.

Who was after us? Was it *one* or many? I still had a lot of questions and not a lot of time for answers. I thought about my 'fellow' Witch Hunters, wondering what they'd feel about me being a witch. Not that I wanted to find out and end up on the pyre, but I was a little excited at the thought of revealing my true self to them when the time came.

To do that, however, I needed to prepare.

To learn my craft.

To perfect my powers.

I sighed, walking around the yard, resetting targets once again.

CHAPTER
NINE

ALEXANDRA

The pungent smell of sage filled my nostrils as I struck the match. Kneeling within the circle of salt, I lit each candle slowly, one by one, their flames dancing in the night breeze. Teddy lit candles around the courtyard as shadows flickered across the moonlit space.

Teddy and I sat cross-legged on large pillows, warm quilts wrapped around our shoulders. With eyes closed in concentration, I uttered the incantation that I knew so well and that Teddy was now learning. The words from my lips fell empty in the night air, the power behind them lost with the loss of my magic, but I said them just the same. I was relying on Teddy to give them the energy needed to conjure my mentor, Cressy.

"Waldo "Cressy" Cress, my deceased mentor, now communicated with me from the other side and appeared when I summoned him. Even though I couldn't conjure him myself, I thanked the Goddess I could still see him. His guidance had been invaluable, his knowledge of ancient magic providing a beacon of hope amid the darkness.

We continued the incantation;

"Heaven to Earth, hear my plea. Bring back he who watches over me.
Goddess and gods of North, East, South, West, allow me to commune with my dear Cress."

The air grew heavy with anticipation. Even without my powers, I could feel the veil between worlds thinning, or at least I could imagine it because I'd done this many times before. Blackjack took up his usual position, pacing around the circle excitedly. A tickle on my neck told me I was no longer alone.

Teddy gasped. I opened my eyes.

"Cressy."

My old mentor stood before me within the circle, faintly luminescent. His wispy form wavered for a moment, then solidified.

"Alexandra. Teddy, how lovely to be summoned by you again." His voice echoed as if from a great distance. Teddy blushed.

"My dear child. How is the Dagon Queen coping in this new world? Are you alright?"

I nodded, unsure where to begin.

Cressy's wise eyes searched my face. "What troubles you, child? Have you not found the handsome Mr. Sheraton?"

I took a deep breath, willing my tears away—no use delaying.

"Not yet, Cressy. And no luck finding a spell to bring my powers back, either."

Cressy nodded, rubbing his chin with a long-nailed finger. "I'm so sorry, my child. I'd secretly hoped that you had good news to share."

I shrugged. "Nothing yet, and the Witch Hunters are being defiant. I've heard of some protests happening in several of the major cities. Nobody wants to see me on the throne. I can't blame them, I guess. Their entire world has been turned upside down."

Cressy nodded. "True. My concern is with *you*, however. Do you have enough protection? Moving to the castle was smart and necessary, but it's not impenetrable."

"I have Teddy here and her hounds. I feel pretty safe. So far, no Witch Hunters have stepped on the castle grounds or even so much as thrown an egg at the windows, so I think I'm safe. So far..."

"Good. I shall rest easier on the other side. But what prompted you to summon me today? You know I cannot help you get your powers back. And I'm hardly a suitable guard dog." Cressy smiled, spreading his arms across his form. Teddy giggled.

"There's been a murder, Cressy. A man found beheaded near Miller's Creek." I described the gruesome scene, sparing no detail, and Carrigan's ghost sighting. When I finished, I let out a heavy sigh.

I shivered. "But who? Or what?"

Cressy's spectral form flickered again as he considered. When he spoke, his voice was grave.

"We must prepare for the worst, Alexandra. This may be the work of Murder himself."

I stared at Cressy, hoping I had misheard. But the grim expression on his translucent face told me I had not.

"Murder?" My voice cracked. I pulled at the vial earring. "As in a demon named... 'Murder'? Who in the heck...?"

Cressy nodded solemnly. "The beheading is his mark. According to the Testament of Solomon, Murder is a headless demon who sees through his breasts and speaks with the voice taken over from his victims. The Testament states that Murder is summoned to appear before King Solomon. He has no head, and he tries to get one by devouring the heads of his victims. Murder grabs heads, cuts them off, and attaches them to himself. And he won't stop at just one…"

A shudder rushed through me. "You've *got* to be kidding me, Cressy. How am I supposed to stop this…*thing?*"

"Without your powers, you are vulnerable to his evil, Alexandra. Be careful."

I groaned, raking my fingers through my hair. Murder was no mere specter to be banished by a few herbs and incantations. Not that I could even *perform* an incantation. Successfully.

He was a demon, ancient and merciless.

"What can I do?" I whispered. "My magic is gone. I'm powerless against him."

"Not powerless." Cressy drifted closer, his misty form enveloping me in cold comfort. "I prefer to look at this as your magic is…' temporarily restrained,' not destroyed. We must unlock it once more."

"From your lips, Cressy. I've been trying everything, reading everything. I'm powerless without someone who can interpret the book or come up with the answer. And now, another demon is on the loose."

Man, I can NOT catch a break!

"Regardless, you must haste. Even now, 'Murder' stalks his next victim.

"Oh, crap on a cracker, Alex. We have to do something!" Teddy wailed.

I gave Teddy a sideways glance. "Would if I could, Ted." I thought of the townspeople sleeping unaware as evil stirred. Carrigan, most of all - her strange new gift left her vulnerable.

"I know I have to stop him, Cressy," I said through gritted teeth. "But how?"

Cressy squeezed my shoulder with his ghostly fingers.

"You will find a way," he assured me. "But you cannot face him alone. You've got to summon the underground witch population for help, Alexandra."

"But, if I do that, then the potential for the Witch Hunters to *hunt* them...Cressy, I can't take that chance."

"You have little choice, my dear. Save the innocents." His form dissolved. The last candle flickered out. Darkness descended on the courtyard. Teddy waved at the empty circle.

"Thank you, Cressy," I whispered, grateful for his continued presence in my life, regardless of whether I could summon him myself.

I stood, Cressy's warnings ringing in my ears.

"Alex, what are we going to do?" Teddy asked.

"What we have to, Ted. Whatever that means..."

Murder was coming, and I'd have to face him.

And this time, I feared for my life.

CHAPTER

TEN

BLAKE

I was ready—mostly.

It had been weeks since learning I was a witch and practicing with my powers. But if I could hazard a guess, I wasn't half bad. Maybe not as good as Alexandra, but since she lost her powers, I could safely say I was much better at this than she was. I chuckled at the thought of her, begrudgingly agreeing, and couldn't wait to tell her.

I was still having a few slip-ups with the aim of my energy, and it made me think I should never play darts or become a professional baseball pitcher. Still, the urgency to get back to Castle Point as soon as possible and help Alexandra end the Witch Hunters spurned me. My aim might not be great, but it's all in the enthusiasm.

My potion and spell casting were coming along like I was an old pro. At least, that's what I thought, anyway. Magma would likely disagree. She helped me sop up several potions that went awry, coating the kitchen walls and floors or setting off the fire alarm. I guess you could say my potion-making skills were more 'Kitchen Catastrophe' than 'Harry Potter.'

I was learning so much about herbs that I imagined Alexandra would be proud of me. I had almost figured out the formula for my favorite shampoo, which I bought from her shop—the one she handcrafted personally.

I even took the winter roses from Magma's garden and tried replicating Alexandra's scent. Trying to mimic someone's scent is a stalker-ish, but desperate times call for desperate measures.

I missed her.

When I finally perfected it, I kept a vial of the scent hidden under my pillow. You know, for those moments when I needed a little whiff of 'Hey, remember the good times before you found out I'm a Witch Hunter' memory.

Every day, I read about and practiced with herbs, potions, and spells until my eyes could barely stay open late into the night. I had two options: become a powerful witch or the ultimate insomniac. I chose the former, and my under-eye bags were a testament to my dedication.

I was with Magma in her cozy kitchen, poring over the family grimoire and preparing another potion to test, when Mom and Dad rushed in.

"Son. We have news from the underground."

Shit.

I winced and eyed them both. "Dad, please find another way to enter a room that isn't so dire and doesn't start with 'news from the underground.' It's never good."

"Sorry, Blake. Our bad." Mom smiled sheepishly and elbowed Dad to apologize.

"What is it? Has something happened to Alexandra?" A ripple of fear tickled my spine. I shook it off. Mom and Magma told me earlier, in training, "If you're going to deal with Witch Hunters, you'll need a spine as strong as a broomstick." I straightened up and waited for Dad to give me the bad news.

"No, Alexandra's fine. For now. But the witch population is in grave danger."

I blew out the breath I'd been holding. "Why? What happened?"

"Because of the news of Alexandra's reign, many of the witches feel confident enough to come out of hiding, admitting their witches to the public. Posting pictures of their rituals on their Facebook profiles and singing praises to the new witch on the throne. Worse, they're taunting the Witch Hunters in person and on social media. The result has been treacherous."

"Treacherous? How so?"

Mom laid her hand on my arm. The warmth of her touch immediately relaxed me. That touch was like a "calm down" button for my brain. "The hunters have revolted against Alexandra's reign and upped the hunts. They are targeting the witches, stripping them of their powers and... killing them."

I closed my eyes and blew out a long breath. Not good. More like very, very, very bad.

"What can we do?"

"We're monitoring the 'chatter.' Hopefully, the witch population clues in sooner than later and keeps silent—but so many of them are sick of having to hide—"

Dad interjected. "Many of them are coming out of hiding anyway and taking their chances. The hunters are being sneaky, however. The witches that were taken had absolutely no clue until it was too late."

I ran a hand through my hair. "What the hell did they think was going to happen? The Witch Hunters would invite them over for tea and cookies? They'd all shake hands and get along? They can't be that naïve!"

Dad paced the tiny kitchen. "With Alexandra—one of their own—in the castle, they've gotten complacent. Thinking they were safe from the hunters."

"Dad, Alexandra won't be able to live with herself if this continues. We have to do something."

Mom, Dad, and Magma agreed.

"You're right, of course. We have to do something soon, Son. Before more lives are lost."

I turned to Magma, my trusted sage and potion master. "I know I'm not much of a potion maker, but I can throw a helluva good energy ball now. Do you think I'm ready?"

Magma brushed my hair from my eyes and smiled. "As ready as you'll ever be."

"Good. Then let's go."

Dad and Mom looked at each other, then at me. "Go? Where?"

"Castle Point."

CHAPTER

ELEVEN

ALEXANDRA

I paced the wide castle hallway, mind racing. A demon was loose in Castle Point. And not just any demon—a demon *called* 'Murder.'

Who the heck named a murderous demon 'Murder' anyway?

Curious as I was to research the origins of this demon, I'd have to leave that for later. Right now, I had to stop him, but how? My powers were gone. And it wasn't like Teddy was a seasoned enough witch to be of any help. Not that I would consider putting her up against a demon of Murder's magnitude, anyway.

And there was absolutely no way I would involve any of the witches on their merry way *out* from the underground. They were in deep enough trouble as it was.

No, it was up to me.

Wasn't it always?

I was but one witch against a creature of nightmares.

Technically, I wasn't even a witch.

Blackjack purred, pressing against my leg, stopping me in my tracks. I reached down absently to scratch his ears. *"Woman, you're carving the stone floor with all this walking. By the Goddess, stop already."*

"Okay, Blackjack. But I have to *think*. How will I get rid of a demon I know nothing about with powers I no longer have?"

Blackjack meowed and gave what looked like a tiny shrug.

I truthfully didn't know either, but my resolve wouldn't let me go down that road. "Don't worry, boy. We'll figure this out." My voice sounded more confident than I felt.

"Oh, goodie. More demon hunting. I'm overwrought with excitement. Can you feel it?" Blackjack peered at me with a bored look. *"If you insist on meddling with demons, could you at least call the good people at 'Demon Hunters' and make us famous? We could use the sponsorships to buy better cat food."*

"Haha. Hilarious, Blackjack. The answer is no." I took a deep breath, steadying myself.

I made a quick plan but had to hurry.

First, I needed to check on Carrigan. Being the only person who'd seen and heard the ghost of the demon's victim, she was vulnerable, an easy target for Murder's insatiable bloodlust. I walked to Teddy's castle wing and rapped on her bedroom door.

"What's up, boss?" She answered sleepily.

"Ted, I need to borrow Draco and Lucius for a walk. Can you glamor them, please?"

"A walk? At this hour? Everything okay?"

"Yeah, everything is fine. Well, not fine, but...I need to chat with Carrigan, and I don't think it's safe for me to leave the castle unattended right now..."

"Gotcha. Say no more. Boys!"

The hounds immediately got up from their carpet in front of the enormous fireplace, the fire inside now a pile of burning embers, and strolled over.

"Good boys. Sit pretty for Mama." Teddy waved an expert hand in their direction, murmuring a glamor spell, turning the nasty-looking hounds into adorable, slobbery Bull Mastiffs.

"Perfect, thanks, Ted. Hey boys. Walkies?" I patted my hip for the hounds to follow, which they happily did, excited to get out and explore despite the late hour.

I hurried across the moonlit parking lot, my boots echoing on the stones. Blackjack and the hounds fell into step beside me.

"Drooling idiots or no, you're taking a colossal risk being out here, woman."

"It's okay, boy," I murmured, though my heart was pounding. He had a point.

"You keep saying that, but I'm not convinced." He bounded ahead.

The town of Castle Point was silent as a tomb as we walked to Carrigan's home. A few street lamps lit the way, shadows dancing ominously. Shivers, both from the chill of the winter air and the frightening shadows, ran through me.

For Goddess's sake, relax, Alex. If anyone were hiding in the bushes, the hounds would smell them and have them on the ground in seconds.

I scolded myself and relaxed, focusing on breathing slowly as we approached Carrigan's small brick cottage. The house was straight out of the story of the three little pigs, the brick house impenetrable by the wolf. I doubted that applied to demons, however. Ivy vines climbed over every square inch. The last fall flowers surrounding her small property were brown or dying with the impending winter chill.

I knew her house was one of many on the Castle Point Haunted House Tours and wondered if she could now see the ghosts supposedly haunting her home. If memory served, Carrigan was not just the Corpse Collector but also a local historian and haunted house tour guide.

I mused at the responsibility put on one person and wondered how she managed it all. I rapped sharply on Carrigan's door. Blackjack slipped into the flower bed and crouched, waiting. The hounds sat obediently behind me.

After a moment, the door creaked open. Carrigan peered out. Wearing a robe and slippers, she was wide-eyed and disheveled as if she hadn't slept in days, which she likely hadn't.

"Oh, Alexandra," she said. "Come in..."

I pushed past her into the vestibule, Blackjack and the hounds at my heels. Carrigan led me into the living room. I recognized the cats I had seen at her office a few days before and wondered how they traveled from home to the office and back again before realizing that Blackjack's back arched —along with every cat in the room—and the hounds started a low growl.

I quickly shuffled the three out the door and told them to sit and wait for me outside. Then I took a chalk from my pocket and promptly etched a protective sigil on the door. Carrigan watched curiously.

"What are you doing?"

"It's a protective sigil. Even without my powers, I can give you *some* form of protection. A Sigil is just the thing," I hoped so, anyway. The gesture made me feel somewhat better, so that was something.

"M'kay, whatever you say. Can I make you a tea—"

"You're in danger," I told her bluntly. "There's a demon called 'Murder' loose in Castle Point. He preys on the innocent...like you." I winced, scolding myself for delivering such lousy news with barely a 'hello.'

Carrigan paled and plopped into a chair, narrowly missing one of her cats.

I rushed toward her. "I'm so sorry, Carrigan. That was a crappy way to tell you, but we have little time. I'm working on a way to stop him, but honestly, I'm afraid you're in danger. You must stay inside for now and not go anywhere alone." I fixed her with a piercing look. "Promise me, Carrigan."

She nodded mutely.

"Good." I turned to leave, then paused. "If you see anything strange, get word to me right away. He will kill again."

"How do you know...?"

I met her eyes, filled with confusion and fear. "You don't need to know. It would be best if you didn't. Keep yourself hidden as much as possible. Can you do that?"

"What about my business? I have a funeral to perform on Saturday..."

"Yes, fine, but ask for extra help from your staff. If you must leave the house, ask Penny or someone you can trust to escort you. Otherwise, stay inside. Promise me?"

She nodded.

I swept out Blackjack and the hounds again on my heels. We had preparations to make before Murder's reign of terror began. And I feared the coming darkness would bring more blood and death to Castle Point.

If only I knew what, how, and when...

TWELVE

BLAKE

A day later, we loaded up the same van my parents kidnapped me in weeks before and headed to Castle Point just before nightfall. The roads were frosty from the early winter chill spurned by the cold northern wind. I pulled my coat—borrowed from Dad and the other clothes I'd been wearing—tighter around me in the back seat, Magma beside me, and stared out the frosty window.

Mom turned in the passenger seat. "Thinking about Alex, honey?"

I nodded. "Always."

Mom gave a soft smile. "We can't wait to meet her. We remember her from when you two were school-age. However, we had nothing to do with her and her family. I believe her mom passed. Is that right?"

"Yeah, I think so." It occurred to me I knew nothing about her mom and how she died. I made a mental note to ask her about it when we had the chance.

If *we had the chance.*

"Now, Son. Don't start thinking the worst before we've even started." Dad peered at me through the rear-view mirror.

"Dad, you're 'reading my thoughts' is getting old." I pushed my thoughts to him.

"Sorry, Son. Old habit." He smiled.

Magma patted my hand. "All will be well, boy." I held my hand over Magmas, welcoming her warmth.

We rode the rest of the way in relative silence. Darkness fell over us the closer we got to Castle Point, but I was grateful for the cover.

I didn't have any reason to be wary. Not yet, anyway. The plan was that I would pretend just to be me, Blake Sheraton, Deputy Sheriff, and Witch Hunter. I would say someone had kidnapped me, but I didn't know by whom or why. Tell them some miraculous story: I woke up in the forest, and finding my way back took me a while. Maybe blame Jeffrey Diebert for the kidnapping. Say that he was probably scared I'd take Penny's powers because I initially discovered she was a witch or some such malarky.

Hopefully, everyone will believe me.

I turned my thoughts back to Alex. A warmth flooded my body, and I shifted uncomfortably in my seat. To say I was excited to see her was the understatement of the century.

I only hoped that she'd be just as excited to see me. I could imagine telling her about being kidnapped by my parents—who weren't dead, by the way—and how I'm a witch, not a Witch Hunter.

That should be interesting.

I chuckled, thinking it was just too outlandish a story for even Alex to believe. I could imagine her saying: "You vanished for weeks, and this is the best excuse you could come up with?"

I couldn't wait to tell her.

More than that, I couldn't wait to kiss her again if she'd let me. I thought of Alex's face, lips, and long, wavy black hair. Immediately, my body heated up from the inside, activating my groin. I squeezed my eyes shut, willing my parts to relax and remembering that Dad was likely reading my thoughts. I'd have to ask Magma for a shielding spell to keep Dad and others out of my head, assuming there was such a spell.

In the meantime, I'd keep my thoughts and damn reactive groin in check.

At least until I saw her again.

I'll be there soon, Alex.

Then, look out.

THIRTEEN

ALEXANDRA

"**A**lex, have you heard?" Penny rushed into the library, her fiery red hair streaming behind her like a comet's tail. Her face flushed and covered in tiny beads of sweat. She doubled over, hands on her knees, panting.

"Hey Penny, nice to see you too. Did you run from home?" I put down the ancient text I had been pouring over, trying to find any information I could on the demon Murder. "And heard what?"

"Witch, you gotta check your emails more often. There's news from the underground, and it isn't good." Penny pulled her crazy hair back into a ponytail and leaned against the desk.

"Not a witch. At least, not at the moment." I replied sourly.

"Witch. Bitch. Pick your term and check your emails."

I eyed Penny as I pulled out my laptop and clicked on the little white envelope on the desktop. The sheer volume of emails I had received in the past twenty-four hours shocked me. Or had it been days? All of them were from fellow witches. "What the...?"

"Yeah, click one and read it." Penny scooped up Blackjack and forced a snuggle.

I clicked on the first one. Reading the first few lines, my hand flew to my mouth as I gasped.

I looked up at Penny. "No. This can't be happening."

"Oh, it is, witchy bitchy. It is."

The witches were coming out from the underground. Because I was now at the helm of the Witch Hunter ship, witches worldwide felt safe enough to come out of hiding, celebrate in groups, and live extroverted witchy lives.

"But.... No. It's not safe, Pen. It's hardly safe for *me* to go outside, and I'm supposedly the Witch Hunter's leader!"

"Yeah, but it gets worse, Alex. The witches who've come out of the broom closet are being snapped up, stripped of their powers, and killed. The Witch Hunter population has completely ignored the fact that Earl Dagon made you their queen. It's business as usual for the sick bastards. You ain't got no R-E-S-P-E-C-T from the hunters, woman." Penny pointed both fingers in the air as she spun in a circle, turned toward the couch, and sat. "And...hey, where'd you go?"

I lay on the floor behind my desk, tears streaming down my face. My body quaked as I grabbed my vial earring and tugged. I stomped my feet on the floor.

Penny peered over my desk. "Temper-tantrum, huh? Classic."

"Pen, what am I going to do?" I cried. "The hunters don't care that I am their queen, witches are dying, and there's a friggin' demon on the loose!"

What else *could go wrong?*

Penny came over, crouched beside me, and helped me up.

"Earl Dagon gave me the crown from beyond the grave, so it isn't like I can count on him to keep the hunters in check."

"True dat." Penny agreed, rubbing my back.

"And my Dagon powers don't work against the hunters."

"They useless, yup."

"And I have no clue how to stop a demon without my powers."

"Yep, no clue."

"And Blake is still missing..."

"Dat boy vanished, yup."

"Agreeing with me is not helping, Pen." I rolled my eyes at her.

"Well, bitchy witchy, seems to me you have to take things step-by-step. What's the first step?"

"I have to email the underground. They need to protect themselves, run, hide..."

"Yes, yes, you do. They'll listen to you, Alex."

"Will they, though? I've lost my witchy powers. I'm the hunter's queen. They likely all think I'm some traitor."

"That's total bull-malarky-pucky, and you know it. You have the witch's respect, Alex, and trust, or they wouldn't be coming out from under their rocks. Tell them you're working on a permanent solution, which you are. Tell them the truth."

Penny had a point, and it was worth a shot. I started a fresh, secured email and typed as Teddy bounced into the library.

"Then, what, Alex? What's next after that?" Penny asked, slapping Teddy's hand in a high-five greeting.

"I must end the Witch Hunter's tyranny."

"Easy Peasy, lemon squeezy—" Penny grabbed Teddy's hand and spun her around.

"Hey Pen, whatcha doin' here—wee!" Teddy squealed.

"I guess you haven't checked your emails either, based on your usual jovial attitude and...wow, fire-red glamor hair. Trying something different, are ya, Ted?"

"Yeah, I got bored with my plain old mousy brown. What's going on?" Teddy nodded toward me. I shut my laptop when I heard the whoosh of the email sending.

"Sit down, Ted," I said, filling her in on the details.

Teddy gasped. "No, no, no. Oh, Alex, that's the worst possible news. Are we even safe?"

A legitimate question. A shiver ran up my spine as I peered behind me, glancing across the library windows into the world where Witch Hunters lived. "We have the hell hounds, so that's something." I nodded toward Lucius and Draco, who bounded over to me upon hearing their names. Teddy hadn't bothered to glamor the hounds today, which was fine. Especially now. The hounds gave another meaning to 'if looks could kill.' These two wouldn't hesitate to rip a hunter into shreds if I asked them to.

"What you got there, Ted?" Penny asked, motioning to the bottle of potion clasped in Teddy's hand.

I answered for her, "Teddy's concocted a new potion, and she wants us to try it."

"A new potion? As in the 'getting our powers back' variety?" Penny took the bottle from Teddy, uncorked it, and sniffed. Her face immediately wrinkled as she corked it and handed it back again, making a gagging sound as she did so. Teddy slapped her on the back and frowned.

"Yes, Pen. I asked Teddy to try concocting anything that might help us regain our powers since the research has turned up nothing." I pushed away the book I had been reading, just about shoving it off the desk.

"Sounds like the perfect opportunity for a break," Blackjack said, leaping off the couch to the floor and strolling past the hellhounds toward the door. He'd gotten used to the hounds—within reason—and accepted that they lived together. Blackjack clarified that they could not *look* in his direction. The hounds obeyed and turned their heads away from the commanding kitty.

"Alright, fine," I agreed, pushing away from the table and rubbing my tired eyes. "But just for a bit. We can't afford to waste too much time."

"What did the cool cat say?" Penny asked, "And why won't you talk to me, Blackjack?" She scooped him up as he made tracks for the door, a couple of tiny toots escaping his back end.

"He said we should take a break, and he's right. It would help if you recharged, Alex," Teddy said soothingly as we walked across the grand hall from the library to her potion workshop. Her hell hounds at our heels, excitedly whining.

"Wait, *you* can hear Blackjack too?" Penny gaped at Teddy, then frowned at Blackjack.

Teddy laughed. "Yep. I guess he decided I could hear him. Probably since I live here and all. Isn't that right, Blackjack?" Teddy gently picked him up and held him close. He tossed a look Penny's way and immediately purred.

"This one doesn't suffocate me like someone *else does..."*

Penny's eyebrows shot up. "Blackjack! I heard that! Aunty Penny would *never* suffocate you, you silly boy!" Penny tried to take him from Teddy's arms, but Teddy ran around her large work table to the door, releasing Blackjack.

83

"Quick! Run!" she yelled after him as he high-tailed it down the hall and toward the kitchen, a sputter of kitty farts trailing behind him.

Penny huffed. "Okay, fine. Let's get this potion business over with."

"I think I might have nailed it this time. This potion should do the trick!" Teddy wiggled like an excited puppy.

"Please tell me it tastes better than the last one," I quipped, trying to suppress a shudder at the memory of Teddy's previous concoction.

"Promise," Teddy winked, handing me a steaming mug filled with a deep blue liquid. A harsh, muddy scent wafted through the air as I took a cautious sip without making a face.

"Wow, this is good," I admitted, feeling the warmth throughout my body as the potion spread through me.

"See? I told you I could do better," Teddy laughed, her eyes sparkling with pride.

"Alright, you've convinced me. Bottom's up!" Penny grabbed a cup of the potion and chugged it. She swallowed it hard, her face contorted as she coughed and sputtered. "I thought you said it was good!" She yelled at me as she grabbed a cloth and rubbed her tongue.

"I lied." Tears burst, and my sides hurt from laughing. "Thanks, Pen. That was just the laugh I needed."

"Sneaky...bitch...witch," Penny said between tongue rubs.

"That'll teach you." Blackjack peered around the door, green eyes dancing.

"Not nice, Blackjack. Hey! You're talking to me again!" Penny put the cloth down and smiled.

"Selectively. Don't get your booty in a bunch." Blackjack winked at me and sat down.

Teddy pouted. "You were fibbing? Not nice, party pooper."

My laughter died down. "Sorry, Teddy. I couldn't help myself."

"Forgiven. Notice anything yet?"

I took a deep breath and stood tall. Wiggling my fingers, I focused my intention on creating a spark.

"Nothing yet. You, Penny?"

Penny grabbed my arm and squeezed her eyes shut, trying to connect with her inner sight. "Nothing here, either."

Teddy bowed her head and pouted. "Gosh dang-it. I thought I had it this time."

I gave her a quick squeeze. "Thank you for trying, Teddy. Really. Thank you."

"Yeah, kiddo. You're the best." Penny hugged her. "Don't give up, though, m'kay? You might nail it."

I agreed, my determination still burning strong but tempered by the support of my friends. "In the meantime, it's back to the books and see if we can figure out how to stop a demon."

"Yes, boss." Teddy and Penny saluted me and yawned as we returned to the library for yet another evening of deciphering text.

May as well. With the loss of witch's lives, there would be no sleep tonight.

Maybe never.

I shuddered and opened The Book.

CHAPTER

FOURTEEN

BLAKE

Castle Point was well under darkness and creeping into the early morning when we arrived. A blanket of fresh snow coated the small town, sparkling off the crescent moonlight. My stomach flipped as we approached Castle Dagon, high on the cliffs overlooking Castle Point.

Alexandra's new home.

Nerves of anticipation pierced every inch of my skin. I was excited and overwhelmed, my head and heart pounding the closer we approached. I couldn't wait to see her.

What if she didn't want to see me?

"I'm sure she'll be happy to see you, Son."

"Reading my thoughts again, Dad? Haven't we talked about this?"

"No, not at all. Just assuming," he smiled at me in the rearview mirror.

"Park just ahead. We'll walk to the castle from here."

Dad pulled into a space near some bushes, and we exited the van. I stretched before practically loping across the street and up the stairs leading to the castle, my parents and Magma following at a much slower pace. I stopped and looked back impatiently.

"We're witches, Son. Not Olympic stair climbers," Dad puffed.

"It's okay, just don't slip, please. There is frost." I whispered. "Meet you at the top." I took steps two and three at a time until I reached the parking lot. Assuming Alexandra closed the museum when she moved in, nothing had changed since the castle was a piece of Dagon history, except for the resident. My heart beat hard in my chest. I wasn't sure it was from the stair climb.

Mom, Dad, and Magma caught up. Time to cloak before getting into view of the security cameras. Mom said her cloaking spell, *"Goddess good, Goddess great, cloak us all to keep us safe,"* waving her hand over us as we disappeared into the blackness.

She had never cloaked me before. The initial sensation was weird, but I didn't feel much different from my natural self once it was done. Although dimly, I could still see my parents and Magma, each a dark, luminescent figure. I could see my hands and feet and feel the winter wind in my hair and the cold against my cheek, but I knew if I were to look in a mirror, I wouldn't see my reflection looking back at me.

"Ok, let's go." I moved toward the door and stared at the lock. As Magma taught me, I pointed a finger at the lock and intended for the tumblers to turn. A tiny spark of light burst from my finger through the lock, and the door popped open in a fraction of a second. Although I knew security cameras had been installed months ago, I crossed my fingers that

Alexandra hadn't installed a door alarm. Opening the door further, I checked it for any connections to the alarm system and found none. Somewhat relieved, I made a mental note to have them installed as soon as possible.

We moved into the grand hallway toward the library and slowly opened the door, mindful of creaks. "Stay in here. I'll go find Alex." The three witches stepped into the library, closing the door behind them.

I rushed to the stairs. Finding Alex in a castle full of wings and rooms could be challenging, but I had my extraordinary new witchy powers set to 'high,' so it should be easy. At the top of the grand staircase, I stopped and centered myself. I could feel several people in the castle. A few below, in what would be the servant's quarters, one to my left, with a couple of...animals? *That must be Teddy and her dogs.* And one to my right, with the small body of an animal curled beside her.

Alex and Mr. Farty Cat.

I bound up the second flight of stairs to the right of the landing—Alexandra's wing. I practically ran past several doors, sensing she was in the room closest to the tower. It made sense; it would be the grandest room with the best view of the ocean and town below.

A room fit for a queen.

I chuckled as I approached the door. Turning the knob slowly, I opened the door and stepped inside, approaching the large, four-poster bed. The moonlight cast a gentle glow through heavy draperies not entirely closed.

My breath caught. There was Alexandra, her beautiful raven black hair splayed out against the pillow, eyes closed, sleeping peacefully, the farty cat curled beside her. I sat on the edge of the bed, my vision blurring with surprising tears, and watched her chest rise and fall with her breath. She shifted slightly, licking her lips and giving a soft moan as she did so.

Those lips I had been longing to kiss for weeks now.

I leaned forward slowly. The scent of rose oil wafted up to me. The same scent I had successfully recreated in Magma's kitchen, the vial of which was tucked into the pocket of my jeans. I lingered over Alexandra's face, breathing her in.

I ducked my head toward hers, wanting so desperately to plant a gentle kiss on her lips, but I stopped short. She moaned lightly and shifted. I pulled back, mesmerized by her beauty. She shifted more, eyes still closed. Her head tossed back and forth on the pillow. As much as I wanted to touch her, to kiss her, I hesitated.

Although we had shared an amazing, intimate moment weeks ago, so many things had changed—for both of us. We were different people now, she a queen, and me, a witch. I couldn't be certain that her feelings for me remained—if she had any feelings at all.

Would she even be happy to see me?

I was about to brush my fingers along her jaw and gently wake her when the farty cat meowed loudly in my ear, a fart blasting from his back end as he did so.

I pulled back from Alexandra as her eyes flew open.

"What the...who's there?" She reached out, slamming her hands into my head, and shrieked, jumping back onto her pillows. "Who's there? Who are you? Earl Dagon? Is that you, you lascivious bastard? F-off!"

"Alexandra, for Goddess's sake, it's me!"

She stopped, her eyes searching. What was she searching for? Couldn't she see me? I...for the love of the

Goddess, in my excitement to see her, I had forgotten the cloak.

"B...Blake? Is that you?"

"Yes, it's me. Hang on." I said the de-cloaking spell my Mother taught me and crossed my fingers it would work.

It did.

Alexandra gasped. "Oh my Goddess, Blake! You're *alive!*" She dove for me, throwing her arms around my neck and planting a thousand kisses on my face. My questions about whether or not Alex would be happy to see me were answered.

"I...can't...believe...you're...okay." She sobbed between kisses, her tears wetting her lips and my face as she did so.

I slid my hands around her back and into her hair, tilting her head back, and closed my mouth over hers. Her response was as I'd hoped: long, slow, and delicious.

After a few moments, she ripped her head back and threw herself onto her pillows again. I quickly crossed my legs, hoping to hide the apparent burgeoning beast.

"Wait. You were cloaked when you came in here. How did you know how to do that? Are you...did you...Oh, my Goddess, you stole a witch's powers! You killed a witch! *How could you!*" Alexandra threw herself at me, beating her fists against my chest. Tears and snot flew. Farty cat swiped at my arm, drawing blood, then bolted from the bed, meowing loudly.

The burgeoning beast rapidly deflated.

"Alex, stop! Let me explain." I grabbed her wrists and held them tight. She started kicking me. I couldn't help but laugh. "Ow, stop that, now!"

"You Witch Hunting *bastard!* You're no better than the rest of them! And I'm your queen! I command you to give up your powers, you smarmy beast!"

"Alexandra! I swear I didn't steal powers from anyone, by the Goddess."

"I...what? You...by the Goddess? Blake, what's going on?" She sat back. I let go of her wrists. She rubbed the redness from them and wiped at her face. I stood up, pacing to the windows. Dawn was breaking. I whipped open the heavy draperies, lighting the room in the glow of early winter, and looked at Alex.

She was radiant. She was breathtaking, even disheveled, stripped of her powers, the weight of the world on her shoulders.

My heart thrummed deep inside my chest, threatening to burst.

"Alex..." I began, sitting on the edge of the bed once again. "I'm a witch."

She crossed her arms and frowned. "I can see that, Blake. Whose powers did you steal?"

I smiled. "Nobody's. I'm a witch. Always have been. I didn't know it. And..."

She uncrossed her arms, her brow furrowed. "Wh... what? And, what?"

"My parents are alive. And also witches."

She leaned back and blew out a breath, sinking into the pillows. "Blake. Explain. Now."

Goddess, I loved it when she was commanding.

I explained.

Everything.

When I was done, Alex said, "That's a pretty tall tale, Sheraton. You leave for weeks, and that's the best you can come up with?"

I laughed a huge, boisterous laugh. "I knew you'd say that. But it's all true. I swear on the Goddess."

She got onto her knees and shuffled over to me. She

91

pushed the hair from my face and kissed my forehead softly. "Wow. Just...wow."

"You're tellin' me." I returned the kiss. "Now, get dressed," I said, lightly slapping her behind. There are people I'd like you to meet."

"Who?"

"My parents."

FIFTEEN

ALEXANDRA

T his man was unbelievable. First, he accosts me while I'm sleeping—okay, that wasn't so bad— then tells me he's a witch whose powers had been bound practically since birth. Okay, that wasn't so bad either.

Pretty cool, actually.

It's great we are finally playing for the same team—sort of. I'd lost my powers and became the Queen of the Order that he had, only a few weeks ago, still belonged to.

My head spun from the irony.

Blake's been missing for weeks and turns up unexpectedly, with parents who are *alive* no less, whom he now wants me to meet.

So...I'm not the only one with a cauldron full of secrets, though I usually wait until the third—or tenth date, should such a date occur, to meet the guy's parents.

I mean, we haven't even *slept* together yet.

Not that I expect we would. He's a Witch Hunter, after all...no, wait.

Scratch that.

Not a hunter.

Just a witch.

Doable.

I smiled at the double entendre as I quickly dressed and joined Blake, waiting for me in the hall. I gasped a little. His handsome features had somehow become...enhanced since I'd seen him last. His hair was a little longer, his eyes a deeper color of fall brown, and his smile was happier, brighter.

He took my breath away.

"This being a witch thing agrees with you," I told him as I approached, pushing a lock of his hair off his ruggedly handsome face.

Dear Goddess, did I bat my eyelashes and blush?

"Get a proverbial grip, woman." Blackjack broke the spell, pushing up against my leg.

Blake smiled, kissed my lips quickly, grabbed my hand, and led me down the hallway, Blackjack in tow. *"Happily reunited with the big doofus. How grand. I wonder if your children will be big doofuses, too."*

"Blackjack, shush."

"Huh?" Blake asked.

"Nothing, never mind."

We walked to the library. Blake opened the door for me and shuffled me inside. There, three people waited. The younger woman, assumably Blake's mom, pulled me into a warm embrace.

"Oh, Alexandra, it's so wonderful to meet you finally. Blake has told us so much about you."

"Oh, he has, has he?"

"All good things, my dear." Blake's dad took my hand in his and shook it firmly. "Lucas Sheraton. Meredith and I are at your service, my queen."

"Lucas...you were a Witch Hunter. A High Commander?"

"Guilty. But only for the good of our kind, I can assure you."

"Blake briefly explained. I have so many questions."

"And we will answer them gladly."

The older Madge—Magma—enveloped me in a warm hug.

"Why don't I arrange breakfast in the kitchen for us all?" I walked to the long, gold-braided rope beside the door and pulled, summoning Malcolm to the library. I invited Lucas and Meredith to sit on the wing-backed chairs while Blake, Magma, and I sat on the comfortable couch in front of the library's central fireplace when Malcolm appeared.

"Your Grace...? You're up ear..." Malcolm stopped, eyeing the company. His eyes widened when they fell on Lucas. I studied them both momentarily.

Was that a look of surprise or recognition?

I'll have to ask later.

I looked at Lucas, but he merely smiled, crossed an ankle over his other leg, and settled into the chair.

"Yes, Malcolm. I have unexpected company. Could you please have the cook serve us breakfast in the kitchen?"

"Uh, why yes, your Grace. But wouldn't you prefer the formal dining room?"

"No, thank you, Malcolm. The sunny kitchen table is fine."

He bowed curtly and backed from the room, again eyeing my guests.

Weird. But then, so is he.

Blake gave a low whistle. "Look at you, all 'Queen of the Castle.' What's it like? Living the dream?"

I busted out a laugh. "Hardly. My life has gotten more complicated in this new role. It does *not* suit me."

"Oh, I think it suits you very well. I always believed it would. When I was a Witch Hunter, that is." Blake smiled and tucked an arm around my shoulders.

It reminded me of our fight in the graveyard when he begged me to embrace my Dagon powers before they stripped me of my own and forced me to do so.

"I think I hate it when you're right."

"At least you agree that I'm right. We're off to a great start." He chucked. I poked him in the ribs with my elbow.

"Does that mean you enjoy being the Dagon Queen?" Lucas asked tentatively.

"Not for a second. But it gives me *some* authority over the Witch Hunters. And that suits me fine. If only I could control the beasts that refuse to acknowledge me as their ruler."

"Yes, we got the news from the underground. Have you communicated with the witches who are exposing themselves to the danger?"

"I've done what I can, yes. The rest is up to each of them. What I need to do is put an end to the hunters. Period."

They all nodded in silent agreement.

"And do you have any plans in that regard?" Lucas asked.

"Nope. My Dagon powers are useless against the hunters. And my witch powers are...gone. So..."

"You have us," Blake reminded me. "And the witch population." Warmth spread through my heart.

"Thank you, Blake. But I refuse to endanger anyone's

life but my own. This is my battle. Besides, someone has threatened your lives once before," I nodded toward Lucas and Meredith, "you had to fake your deaths to escape. Why would I endanger you now? Do you know who was after you all those years ago?"

Lucas shook his head. "We've been over this so many times. We do not know, but the death threats kept coming..."

"It must have been hard to leave Blake behind." I looked at Blake, patting his leg. He squirmed in his seat, his head bowed. The lavender-mint shampoo scent wafted toward me. I breathed in deeply. If he were *my* son, there was no way I'd leave him behind...for anything. The Sheraton's either had a significant reason or...they didn't care for Blake as much as...I did.

Meredith spoke up. "It was a horrible time. Of course, we hated leaving our boy so much, but we felt the only way to protect *him* was to disappear. So he could live a normal life."

I laughed softly. "I'd say it's been anything *but* normal. Living under the Witch Hunter's rule..."

"I disagree," Blake injected, half-smiling. "Becoming a Witch Hunter brought me the acceptance and family I needed when I needed it most."

"It probably saved his life," Lucas agreed.

"How so?" I asked.

"Well, if someone were after us for *being* witches, they would have their eye on Blake, too. They wouldn't have seen any such activity because we had bound his powers, and it has convinced them he wasn't a witch when he joined the order."

I nodded my head slowly. "And Blake only joined the hunters because his father was a hunter..."

"Yes." Blake shifted beside me, pulling me closer, causing my insides to ripple with warmth and a hint of desire. "I didn't know we were truly witches. I was following in my father's footsteps. Plus, Gordon Roberts was my mentor and friend. He took me under his wing after my parents 'death' and encouraged me to join."

I considered this for a moment. "Had you ever suspected Sheriff Roberts of sending the death threats?"

Lucas pursed his lips. "We considered it, but he was our good friend, so I think we would rather assume not..."

I nodded. "Of course. There's a world of hunters out there...could've been anyone."

"Yeah, true," Blake shifted, "but now that I know the truth, I don't think we should let our guard down and trust that Robert *wasn't* involved."

Lucas sat back and crossed his arms. "I hate to argue with you, Alexandra, but this is *our* battle as a collective. You are not alone. Never were, never will be."

I blinked away the sudden spike of tears. "Thank you. That means so much to me. You do not know. Aside from Teddy and the hellhounds living with me, I've felt very much alone."

"Great idea, having Teddy move in with you." Blake rubbed my back. I closed my eyes, warming to his comforting hands. "But you have to have door and window alarms installed ASAP. It was way too easy for us to creep in and surprise you. Any Witch Hunter with stolen cloaking powers could do the same."

"Yes, good point. I've relied solely on Teddy and her hounds, partly as company, partly as protection, and partly to help me find the damn spell that will return my powers —if there even is one. We have been trying to crack the Witch Hunter's Book but can't find any interpretation, and any Witch Hunter who *may* know how to interpret it refuses to step forward and help." I blew out a breath.

"Well, my queen. You are in luck." Lucas smiled.

"I am?" My heart skipped a beat, then went full staccato.

"Yes, indeed. We brought an interpreter." He pointed to Magma.

She smiled.

CHAPTER
SIXTEEN

BLAKE

Alexandra suddenly burst into tears, which were completely unexpected.

"Hey, hey. It's okay." I rubbed her back, pulling her closer to me. She buried her face in my shirt and sobbed.

"It's just...you do not know how...difficult...and lonely... and scared I've...been. And frustrated." She said between sobs.

I was out of my element. I'd seen girls cry–usually when I'd handcuffed them for petty department store theft, but this was different.

This was Alex.

I'd seen Alexandra in every shade of pissed there is, and I'd seen her use her strength. But she had never shown such vulnerability. This was an extra layer I hadn't expected to peel so soon. One that I wasn't yet accustomed to but wholly appreciated. I hugged her closer.

Magma pulled a tissue from the box on the coffee table

and held it to Alex's nose, like a mother with her small child.

"Blow." She directed.

Alex obediently blew. Magma tucked the tissue away and grabbed more to wipe Alex's eyes. I thought the entire scene was sweeter than honey as I watched Magma rub Alex's back.

"Thank you," Alex managed as she grabbed another tissue and blew her nose. "I'm sorry, I'm so embarrassed. I guess I haven't realized how stressed I've become."

Mom smiled, her voice nearly a whisper. "You've been through something none of us have experienced, Alexandra. You're allowed to have emotions."

"I know, but that's not like me at all. I'm the one people come to who are emotional. I'm the one who's supposed to hold it together. Help everyone."

"Well, as I just said, you aren't alone." Lucas reminded her.

Alex nodded. "Thank you. I miss my powers. Aside from that, being unable to interpret the book has been the most frustrating thing I've ever experienced." She turned to Magma. "I hope you can help."

Magma tilted her head, her long silver hair falling around her shoulder. "I know the language, my dear, but I've never had the opportunity to read The Book. Hopefully, we will find the answers within its pages."

"Sheriff Roberts said there isn't a spell to help me regain my powers. Not that he knew of, anyway. He said the only part of the book he knew was the spell to *strip* a witch of her powers, not return them."

"Well, he's not lying." Dad piped up. "I was only taught certain spells from the book myself. I was learning more—before we had to go into hiding."

"Who was teaching you the language?" Alex asked.

Dad nodded toward Magma. "This lady, right here."

Alex turned to face Magma. "Who taught you?"

Magma's lips shaped a large, mischievous grin. "My lover."

I sat back hard against the cushions. "Excuse me? Magma! You've been holding out on me. I didn't know you had a husband."

"No, I said lover." She pointed a crooked finger at the sky. "I never had a husband. And I couldn't marry my lover."

"Dear Goddess, Magma. Why not? Was he already married? Please don't keep us in suspense. Who was he?" I pleaded.

"His name was Bartholomew Bardon."

I paused, my brow knitting together. "You've *got* to be kidding me!"

Magma shook her head, her delightful grin spreading.

"Who's Bartholomew Bardon?" Alexandra asked, looking from Magma to me.

Magma answered. "He was a fifth-level High Commander of the Sacred Order of the Witch Hunters."

I felt Alexandra stiffen beside me at the same time I did. "He was a what?" we croaked.

Dad laughed. "It's true. Bartholomew had reached the highest level of the Order. No one has coveted the position since his passing—what—thirty years ago?"

Magma smiled and nodded. "A little longer."

"Thirty years ago? Dad, did you become High Commander around then?"

Dad grinned. "Yes, Bartholomew granted me the position before his passing. We were good friends. Not as good as he and Magma, however," he winked at the old Crone.

"Magma, how long were you and Bartholomew a 'thing'?" I asked.

Magma's eyes sparkled. "Our love affair started over fifty years ago and ended when Bartholemew crossed over…"

Alex sat upright. "Wait. Over fifty years ago? Around the time the witches went underground?"

Magma nodded, again smiling in her mischievous way. "Yes, that's right, child."

"So," I began, "were you trying to infiltrate the Order by being with him? Or was it something else?"

"We fell in love," Magma stated simply. "He was going to steal my powers for himself, but he couldn't do it." Magma winked. "It was his idea for the witches to hide—to go 'underground.' And it was also his idea to name your father his successor and change the rules of the Order. Only teach the hunters the witch-stripping spell. Only that. He knew that, with the witches underground, learning the spell wouldn't be of much use anyway, but he had to continue to appear as the High Command, lest he have to answer to Earl Dagon himself. Hunters who already knew the language were also silenced; most have since crossed over."

I peered at her. "Magma. This is a massive piece of news. I didn't know that you, Bartholemew, and Dad were in cahoots. Wait…did you cast a love spell on Bartholomew?"

Magma merely tapped her crooked fingers and whistled, "Way Down Upon the Stony River."

"Why, you devious little…" I smiled, then reached across Alexandra to high-five the wonderful crone.

"Magma. I'm completely speechless." Alex started, "If it's okay with you, I need to hug you right now." Alex choked back her tears, gently squeezing the small woman, who happily hugged her back, although not so gently.

Malcolm entered the library, head bowed, avoiding our eyes. "Breakfast is served, your Grace." Then pivoted and marched toward the kitchen.

"Where'd you find Lurch?" I asked Alex.

"He worked for Mr. Fellows, the museum curator before I arrived. I keep him and several of the original staff on to maintain the castle." She led us toward the kitchen.

"He's got a 'weird' vibe. You sure he's a 'good guy'?"

Alexandra laughed, the infectious laugh I'd grown to love. "He's harmless. Just a unique individual."

"If you say so..." I admired the large, sunny kitchen. The cook was busy cleaning up as Malcolm served us, just as Teddy bounded into the kitchen with her hellhounds.

"'Morning Alex! Oh, and...Blake? Oh my Goddess, is that you? EEEEEE!" Teddy rushed over to me, barely letting me stand up from the table before launching into my arms and squeezing me around the neck.

"Hey, Teddy." I laughed.

"Oh my gosh, oh my gosh, oh my gosh—you're *alive!*" She dropped to the floor and reached up, grasping my face in her tiny hands. "Just look at you...all alive and stuff. Alex, did you know Blake is *alive?*"

Alex laughed. "Yeah, Ted. I'm aware."

"Ain't that just *something?*" Teddy asked, releasing my face and flopping down onto a kitchen chair. "What the heck happened to you? And who are these people?"

I looked at Mom, Dad, and Magma, frozen in their seats, staring at Teddy's dogs.

No, wait. Not dogs.

My heart rattled. "Holy crap, what are hell are *those?*" I

pointed toward the giant, gray, drooling, snarling beasts sitting obediently close to the table.

"Oh, that's Lucius and Draco. My Hellhounds." Teddy smiled and cooed at the enormous beasts.

"Um, Teddy," Alex chuckled. "Could you maybe...you know...glamor the hounds for our guests?"

"Oh! Duh! Sorry. My bad. We're all so used to seeing them in all their natural glory." Teddy swept her hand in a circle above her head, swirling the hound's alter-ego Bull Mastiff glamor into effect. "I forget they look a little dangerous. They're perfect pups, I promise. Unless you're a Witch Hunter. Wait..." Teddy stared at Blake, wide-eyed. "You're a hunter! And they aren't attacking you. What the heck n' heck?"

I laughed. "Not a hunter, Teddy. I'm a witch."

"Oh, well then. That's good." Teddy dove into her eggs.

We all looked at each other. Alex piped up. "Did you hear that, Ted? Blake is a witch."

"Uh-huh. Dang, these eggs are good. Complimento's to el' Chefo," then she stopped, mid-chew. "Wait...Blake's a what?"

We all laughed. "There it is..." Alex giggled. "Blake can tell you his story."

Mom took a sip of coffee. "Interesting...beasts, Teddy. You'll have to tell me how you came to...own them... sometime."

"Oh, sure! Be happy to. Who are you?" Teddy asked, glancing across the table, yellow egg yolk dribbling from her lips.

I laughed and introduced everyone. Alexandra and I caught Teddy up on what happened in the past few weeks. When she got to the part about Magma being able to interpret The Book, Teddy's high-pitched squeal forced us all to cover our ears and laugh.

The scene was delightfully 'normal'. A family gathered around the breakfast table, laughing, talking, and enjoying each other's company.

If only I could ignore the tiny spikes of doom tickling the back of my mind...

SEVENTEEN

ALEXANDRA

T could barely eat breakfast, my stomach and mind whirring with the possibility that today might be the day I would regain my powers.

As shocked and relieved as I was that Magma could interpret The Book, I was also...nervous. What if Sheriff Roberts was right and there *was* no spell? What would I do then?

I tried endlessly to push the thought from my mind as I finished breakfast, hardly taking the time to appreciate that Blake and his parents were alive and sitting in my kitchen.

One big happy family bound by magic.

Except for me.

The magic-less.

*One of these things is not like the other...*I sang silently.

Tears sprung every time I thought about it. I blinked them away before anyone noticed.

Malcolm cleared the dishes as we returned to the library to dive into The Book. I studied his exaggerated features before leaving, watching to see if he looked at Lucas in that weird way he had earlier, but he avoided eye contact with everyone.

It's not much different from every day—just his usual stoic weirdness.

I had to slow my steps to match those of my guests. Lucas, Meredith, and Magma asked for a tour of the castle. Of course, I complied. They were my guests, and although Lucas had been in the castle frequently as the High Commander, it had been over twenty years since he walked across the threshold, and he was curious if there was anything new.

They were studying the paintings, armor, and other Dagon memorabilia I had yet to remove from the castle and destroy.

I didn't plan on staying long.

Once I have my powers back, I'll turn this into a museum of remembrance of the Witch Trials to benefit those families who lost their loved ones at the Witch Hunter's hands in the past 400 years.

"Alexandra, this painting..." Lucas nodded toward the large painting of Evelyn of Cumbria on the wall leading to the central courtyard. "I've seen it before, of course, but naturally, I didn't see the resemblance between you, young Alexandra Heale, and...her. It's uncanny."

I nodded, clasping my hands behind my back. "Uncanny, because it *is* me. I'm Evelyn incarnate."

Magma, Meredith, and Lucas audibly gasped. I felt Blake stiffen beside me. They all knew the meaning behind it. Evelyn was a witch who spurned Earl Dagon, refusing his love and sending him into the infamous rampage that set him on the course to rid the world of its witch population.

Not my best moment in history.

"Oh, sweetheart..." Meredith breathed. "Are you sure?"

"Oh, yes. My mentor, Waldo Cress, confirmed it. He's been my mentor through several of my past lives."

"Waldo Cress? I remember him. Strange fellow. Is he a witch? I don't recall him being part of the underground..." Lucas asked.

"Yes, he *was* a witch. He crossed over years ago. He was never part of the underground. His sole purpose for being here was to mentor me."

"Oh, I'm sorry, sweetheart," Meredith said, "but I'm glad you had *someone* to mentor you. But, I have a question..."

"Shoot."

"You said he was your mentor through several of your past lives...?"

"Yes, that's right."

"Well, how would he even know to find and mentor you? He would've been reincarnated himself, no? How did he connect with you?"

"When I said he was my mentor, I meant...*he*, Waldo Cress, mentored me. He always knew who I would reincarnate to, and he'd be waiting..."

Blake tilted his head. The shift in his hair releasing the lavender-mint scent, taunting me. "You mean, he was...old? As in...immortal?"

"Old, yes. Immortal, no. A demon killed him..."

"What?"

"No!"

"But how?" Everyone spoke at once.

"It's a long story. If it's okay with you all, I'll save that for another time?"

"Of course, dear. I'm sorry, I didn't mean to pry."

Meredith held me by my shoulders. "I understand from Blake that your mother is gone as well?" Meredith asked.

"Mom! That's prying." Blake scolded.

I paused. It wouldn't hurt anything to tell them now, would it? "It's okay, Blake. My mother is alive."

Blake looked at me questioningly. "I thought you told me she had passed?"

"No, you asked if she was gone, and she is."

"I don't get it."

I took a deep breath. "My mother has lived under a demon's curse at the Lexington County Sanatorium since my late teens. The same demon that killed Cressy."

The room fell silent. You could practically hear the castle breathing.

"Alex," Blake started, "this is unbelievable. Is there anything we can do?"

I considered this. "For my mom, possibly. It's too late for Cressy. Regardless, as with everything else, the witch community comes first, and my need to regain my powers."

Lucas asked, "Any idea who the demon is that did this to your family, and who summoned it?"

"No," I shook my head, "I was too young and too new to the world of demons. I have no clue how to find out and stop it."

Blake wrapped a comforting arm around my shoulders, silently leading me away from the painting. Lucas eyed the large, heavy wood doors leading to the courtyard. I had hammered large spikes into a long wood plank across the door. After surviving the ceremony that stripped Penny and my powers, I shut the doors forever. Thankfully, he didn't ask about them.

We finally arrived back at the library. I rushed over to the glass case where I'd kept The Book—unlocked since I'd had it out of its case every day since arriving. I placed the heavy book on the large, ornately carved desk and invited Magma to sit comfortably. Magma smiled, grabbed a pillow from the couch, and placed it on the seat, giving her more height to study its pages.

Lucas, Meredith, Teddy, and the hounds settled into the comfy couch to hear Teddy's story of acquiring her hounds while Blake stoked the fire in the central fireplace. It was all so typical and inviting, just as breakfast had been. My heart warmed, and I wanted to join them, but pouring over the book with Magma in search of a reversal spell took precedence. I tried not to hover, so I assisted as a note-taker.

Magma knew the language but never could read The Book of the Order of Witch Hunters, so thankfully, she was as eager as I was to learn the content within its pages.

Just as we were about to dive into The Book, Penny, and Carrigan busted through the library door. Lurch—I mean, Malcolm—right behind them.

"I'm so sorry, your Grace. They insisted..."

I raised a hand. "It's fine, Malcolm, thank you. What's up, Pen? Carrigan? Are you okay?"

"No, no, I'm not okay. There's been another murder. Just as the last—a headless victim." Carrigan paused, glancing at the eyes staring back at her. "I'm so sorry for interrupting...I...Penny said you'd want to know..."

"Yes, she'd want to know," Penny interjected. "Company or no...wait...Blake?" Penny gawked at Blake, leisurely sitting on the couch, grinning.

"Hey, Penny. Nice to see you alive and well."

Penny stood firm, hands on hips, clearly stunned. "You're alive and well, too, I see. And you brought more Witch Hunters for backup? Here to steal Teddy's powers now, are you?" Steam was practically boiling off her red face.

I bolted to Penny's side. "Penny, no, Blake's not a Witch Hunter. He's an ally, remember?"

"I remember my powers being stripped by one of his kind; that's what I remember."

Blake stood up. "Penny, I'm not a Witch Hunter. I'm a witch. These are my parents, Lucas and Meredith, also witches, also alive and well." He clasped his hands behind his back and forced a smile. "I'm truly sorry that they have stripped your powers, Penny. I take responsibility for that, and I hope you'll be able to forgive me..."

"You're sorry that stripped my powers, and I *almost died*? And what kind of bull-pucky is this 'witch' business? What are you trying to pull, hunter? Alex, you believe this load of crap?"

"It's all true, Penny. Take a breath and sit down. I'm sure Blake would be happy to explain." Penny reluctantly sat, pulling Teddy closer to her in a protective, smothering embrace while I led Carrigan to the other side of the round room to chat.

"Carrigan, tell me what happened? Did you see the ghost of the latest victim?"

Carrigan took a shaky breath and nodded. "Yes. And it spoke to me, but, just like last time, I don't remember what it said."

"Hmm. Likely the same as the other one had before, but we can do some hypnosis around that, to be sure."

Carrigan nodded. "I've been able to identify the victims now, based on missing persons reports and jewelry. It's been tricky, not having a head or even dental records."

"Oh, that's good though, I guess? Give the families some relief?"

Carrigan nodded again. "Yes, and allow them time to grieve and plan the funerals. But I wish I could answer their questions about *why* the murders happened. The Castle Point Sheriff's Department doesn't seem to know, and I can't tell them it's demon-related. They'll have my license!"

"The Sheriff and most of the deputies—probably all of them—are Witch Hunters, so they're well versed in all things demon-related. That being said, I don't want you to deal with them at all. Leave that to Blake. You go about your funerary business, and if there are any more messages from ghosts, let me know. We'll have to do a hypnosis session to dig deeper into this, if that's okay with you?"

"Yes, for sure. Other than planning these funerals, I'm free. I've been sticking close to home, like you asked. I called Penny first, and she insisted we come to see you." Penny's boisterous roar of laughter came from the other side of the room. Blake was regaling her with stories on his crappy fireball energy throwing.

Lucky bastard. At least he has *fireball energy to throw.*

I rubbed Carrigan's arm absently and offered a small smile. "She was right. It's fine. Can you tell me the names of the victims? Maybe it will help to figure out why they were targeted."

"Sure. Mel Gallagher and Dale Morris."

Lucas stood, whipped around, and interrupted Blake mid-sentence. "Did you just say Mel Gallagher and Dale Morris?"

Carrigan turned toward him, wide-eyed. "Yes. They are the recent beheading victims."

I peered at Lucas. "Why? Do you know them?"

Lucas's face fell, flushing white. "They're both witches." He sat down hard in his chair. "And long-time friends of ours—until we had to run. They, too, were trying to infiltrate the Order, but in other ways, not by being one of them."

"Witches?" I came closer. "So, the demon, Murder, is targeting witches? But why?"

Lucas shook his head. "I do not know."

Blake piped up. "Do you know if they stripped their powers in the process?"

I shook my head. "No idea and I have no clue how we could even find out. Except for what Cressy—my mentor—has said." I sat at the hearth. Carrigan joined me.

"What did your mentor say?" Meredith asked.

I relayed Cressy's information about this demon.

"Doesn't sound like he's after their powers, then." Blake shook his head, his brow furrowing. "Just after them."

"But why them in particular?" Carrigan asked. "I mean, if the demon is after witches, then I'm glad I'm off the list of potential targets, but still...why them, and...who's next?"

Everyone shook their heads or shrugged.

"Maybe the better question is, who summoned the demon?" Magma asked. "It would have to be someone powerful. Summoning a demon isn't easy."

"Maybe it was whoever threatened your life, Mr. Shera-ton." Teddy nodded toward Lucas.

There was a pause as we all considered this.

"Possibly," Lucas said slowly, "Although we don't know who that is, we just know it was someone or more than one someone, and they got too close. So that leads us back to square one. Who's behind the demon? And how do we find out?"

Carrigan piped up. "Hypnosis? Could we try digging a little deeper this time? Maybe the ghosts have told me more than I thought they did."

"Good plan, Carrigan." I nodded. "Let's do it."

Everyone shifted around the room, giving Carrigan her choice of seating. She lay on the couch. I sat on the coffee table beside her. Meredith stayed nearby, pad and pen ready to take notes.

"Okay, Carrigan, just like last time, remember?"

Carrigan nodded and closed her eyes.

"Good. Take a deep breath, relaxing down..." I slowly counted her down into a restful state of hypnosis. I knew she was there when her breathing shifted and became shallow. "Carrigan, can you return to when you saw the second headless ghost, please? Remember that you are perfectly safe. You are just observing and listening to what the ghost says."

Carrigan paused, shifting and fidgeting a little. "Okay, I'm there."

"Good. Can you see him?"

"Yes. The poor man. I can feel his pain. He was so frightened." A tear trickled down Carrigan's temple.

"Can you feel his pain, even now, when he's not in front of you?"

Carrigan nodded.

A thought occurred to me. If Carrigan could still feel the ghost, she could likely summon him. If not to the room, at the very least, to her psyche. And not just one ghost, but both. "Carrigan, can you ask both of the spirits of these men to be in our presence now?"

Carrigan nodded. "Yes." The room fell silent as the grave. "Ok, they are here."

In my periphery, I noticed Teddy and Penny glancing around the room, but the spirits of the two men weren't there. They were linked to Carrigan, so she was the only one who could see them in her mind. I assumed it was because of her newfound ability and not from a direct connection, but I'd have to work that out later.

"Carrigan, can you ask them for more details about their murders?"

"I can try."

"Okay, good, thank you. Please ask them if they saw who murdered them."

Carrigan fell silent momentarily, then said, "They don't know."

"Did they have any warning?"

She shook her head, her thin, brown hair rustling against the pillow. "No, well, yes. They felt something cold. Like a...a...blade, maybe? Or a sword? Against their necks, then...nothing."

"Did they hear any voices? Had the demon said anything before taking their heads?" I shifted, a little uncomfortable on the table but also disgusted by the questions I had to ask.

"Just...just what the ghost told me before...both ghosts, actually..."

"Can you ask them to repeat that, please?"

Carrigan spoke. Her voice was monotone and deep. "'*Murder has risen, and Murder shall reign, and Murder shall take another again. You have been warned.*'"

Blake ran his hand through his hair. The scent of lavender and mint filled my senses. I'd have to bind his hands so he couldn't distract me with that anymore.

"Alex," he whispered. "Can you ask her for more details about who might be behind this?"

Hearing Blake's question, Carrigan answered, "They don't know."

"Okay, thank you, Carrigan. Is there anything else that the spirits think we should know?"

Carrigan considered this, her head slowly rolling from side to side as if looking from one ghost to another. "No, that is all."

"Okay, thank you." I counted her out of hypnosis and let her relax for a few minutes on the couch.

Blake pulled me aside.

"I think it's time I head to the station and return to work. Maybe I'll be able to find out more."

"You're going back to work?" My voice squeaked.

"Yes, that's the plan. We came up with some dumb excuse as to why I was gone. Pointing blame at Jeff Deibert, since he was the one who captured Penny after I..."

"After you turned me in. Asshole." Penny injected with a sly smile, overhearing Blake's plan. "But, since hearing your story... I guess I can forgive you."

Blake beamed. "Thank you, Penny. That means a lot. We'll get your powers back, I promise."

Penny waved a hand. "Meh. Don't make promises you can't keep, Sheraton."

"Okay." I clapped. "Off to work you go, Blake. The rest of us have work and a book to read, right, Magma?" I grinned.

"Magma can interpret the book?" Penny asked, "Finally! I was so sick and tired of studying that stupid thing. Oh Goddess, I can relax now..."

"*Hardly.*" I wagged a finger at her. "All hands on deck, Pen. Until we solve these murders and get our powers back."

Penny flopped on the couch beside Carrigan and slid down the seat with a frustrated sigh, her long, wavy hair trailing. "*Fine.* Better have Lurch re-stock the Cheetos. I have a feeling it's gonna be a long one."

Everyone laughed.

CHAPTER
EIGHTEEN

BLAKE

My heart was thudding as I stepped into the Sheriff's department. I paused, hand on the door, and took a deep breath, willing my heart and emotions to calm down.

Large Larry was on the phone, taking notes on a case. He barely glanced at me but dropped the phone when he realized it was me.

"Hey, Larry." I saluted and pushed the gate to the noisy, boisterous bullpen open. The noise of the deputies shouting, talking, and laughing immediately died.

Then, they simultaneously let out a 'whoop'.

Suddenly, the guys surrounded me, patting me on the back, asking questions, giving me awkward bear hugs, and shaking my hand.

It was a lot.

"Sheraton!" Boomed Sheriff Gordon Robert's commanding voice. The rest of the fray broke away, allowing the Sheriff's approach. His face was stony, his usual thick lips a thin line. He peered at me, then his face broke into a wide smile. "Where the hell have you been, you son-of-a-bitch?" He grabbed one hand to shake while vigorously patting me on the back with another. "We've been looking everywhere and one step away from calling the military to find you!"

"I'd be happy to tell you, sir." I smiled as he led me to his office and shut the door. The bullpen ignited in its usual boisterous noise the second the door closed.

"Sit, please. Can I get you a coffee?" Gordon didn't wait for a reply as he poured two mugs of coffee from the carafe on his credenza, handing one to me.

"Thanks." I took a sip of the hot courage. "Well, it's quite a story, sir."

Gordon sat in his chair and leaned back. "I'm all ears, Blake."

I took a ragged breath, willing my body to relax. The truth of the situation was not lost on me. I was a witch, sitting three feet away from a Witch Hunter.

Wow, was this what Alexandra felt like when she was near me?

I tried to hide a shudder.

"Well, don't keep me in suspense, Sheraton. What happened to you, and where have you been?" Gordon eyed me.

He suspects something.

I tried to hone in on his thoughts but hadn't mastered that ability—yet.

Of course, he suspects something, you idiot. You vanished without a trace, disappeared for weeks, and suddenly reappeared, fine and dandy.

"Well, sir..." I cleared my throat. "They kidnapped me."

Gordon leaned forward. "Kidnapped? By whom?"

"That's the question, sir. I don't know. I never saw my kidnappers. Woke up in a forested area pretty far north of here, near the Canadian border."

Gordon peered at me. "You heard nothing? They never spoke to you?"

"Uh, no, sir. They knocked me out. I woke up later—days later—in the forest. I had to find my way out. It took a while."

"Intriguing. They didn't leave you with any supplies? No phone?"

I shook my head. "No, sir. Nothing. They left me for dead."

Yeah, that sounded good.

Gordon let out a low whistle. "How'd you survive?"

Okay, imagination, let's roll. And hope he believes me.

"I found a small river, so I had plenty of water. I followed the river until I came to a road. Some people found me and took me in."

"How long were you there?"

"Weeks, sir."

Gordon's eyes narrowed. "They didn't have a phone? You couldn't call to say where you were?"

Shit.

"Uh, no, sir. We were out in the middle of nowhere, at their cabin. Also, I wasn't well. I was...starving..."

Gordon leaned back in his chair and whistled. "You look pretty darn good for a starving man."

My eyes flicked to my boots. "Well, I had a few pounds I could stand to lose. I've eaten nothing but carbs since, so..."

Gordon peered at me and slowly nodded. "Quite the story."

Shit. Did he believe me?

I could feel my hair dampening with beads of sweat.

"Yes, sir. It was quite the time. Once I was well, they took me to the nearest town. I hitched rides all the way home."

He nodded again, just as slowly as before. I took a few gulps of my coffee, my hand shaking slightly. "Why didn't you go to the local authorities? Someone who could let us know you were okay?"

Dammit

"Uh, I...tried that, sir." I tried to get my swallowing under control. "They didn't believe my story. I can't say I blame them. It's pretty wild. They drove me to the county line. From there, I thumbed a ride from a trucker who took me the rest of the way. I slept most of the trip. By the time I woke up, we were in Castle Point."

Even I was believing my line of bullshit.

Gordon raised an eyebrow and pushed on. "Who do you think kidnapped you, Blake?"

I shook my head. "I don't know, sir. I've been wracking my brain since gaining consciousness in the forest. Jeff Delbert is the only person I could think of that would want me out of the way."

A harsh laugh burst from Gordon's chest. "That's ridiculous. Why would Jeff want to kidnap you?"

"Because I was the one who figured out that Penny's a witch, sir. He wanted her powers for himself and was afraid I'd get in the way when the time came to take them."

"Preposterous. I had already sanctioned his kill. He had no reason to come after you after the fact."

I cringed at the word 'kill'. Penny and Alexandra had both come so close. They'd both be gone if it weren't for Alex's Dagon powers.

And I'd have no reason to return to Castle Point...or live.

"Well, that's the best I've come up with, sir. I can't think of any other reason someone would want me...dead."

Gordon looked out the window, his lips pressed into a line, then turned to face me. "Well, I'm just glad you're back, Sheraton. Things have been a little crazy around here. The Earl himself has named Alexandra Heale Dagon Queen. Were you aware?"

"I'd heard, sir, yes. Pretty big news."

"Yes. Have you seen her since you've been back?"

I quickly shook my head. Maybe too quickly. "Uh, no, sir. I got cleaned up and came straight here."

Gordon nodded. "Well, our new queen has put the kibosh on the hunts, which has caused quite the stir. A lot of hunters refuse to accept her reign. Every police station nationwide—no, worldwide—has been working overtime. There have been many riots and a few murders of the witches that have been crazy enough to come out from the rocks they've been hiding under."

I nodded. My stomach lurched. "Sir, can I ask you a question?"

"Of course."

"What's your opinion? About Alex's reign, that is."

Gordon looked down into his mug, then back up at me. "She's our queen, Blake. What choice do we have but to obey Earl Dagon's rule?"

I nodded. My witchy senses were on high alert. "Sorry, sir, but that doesn't answer my question. What do *you* think about Alexandra being named Dagon Queen?"

Gordon practically slammed his mug onto his desk and let out a ragged breath. "It is what it is, Blake. I took an oath to uphold the law when I became an officer and an oath to uphold Dagon's rule when I became High Commander."

"Agreed. But, personally? What's your take?" I pressed.

Gordon peered at me, his eyes hooded under thick, graying brows. "She's our queen. She makes the rules under Earl Dagon's command. Why are you so concerned with my feelings on the subject, Blake? Do you think I'm part of the problem? Or do you plan to continue a relationship with the queen and are concerned with what I might think?"

I clasped my hands in my lap. "No, sir. I don't think you're part of the problem. And, just to be clear, I never *had* a relationship with Alexandra. We got close, but that was all an effort to gain more knowledge of her powers. I'm just asking friend to friend."

Gordon nodded, accepting the half-truth. "You're asking if I'm on her side?"

"Yes, sir. I guess I am." I briefly closed my eyes, willing my senses to pick up on whether anything Gordon said was true or a lie.

"I'm on her side, Sheraton, as we should be. To go against the queen would be to go against Earl Dagon himself. Dead ruler or not, he's our ultimate leader. What he says goes. Period."

Maybe it was because I *wanted* to believe him, or he was telling the truth. I felt his honesty flood through me. I let out a relieved sigh.

Also, the question of who threatened my parents' lives, forcing them to fake their deaths, was still unanswered.

"Sir, can I ask you another question?"

"Of course. Shoot."

"Do you, or did you, have any idea who it was who killed my parents?"

Gordon peered at me, his fingers strumming against his coffee mug. "That was years ago, Blake, and something we've been over repeatedly. You know it was a witch."

I picked my words carefully. "Yes, that's what I was always told, but do you believe that?"

Gordon pulled his mug to his lips and took a long gulp. "Of course, I believe it. Why would you even ask?"

I swallowed hard. "Well, I just wondered. I know you were...close...to my father. You were next in line for High Commander..."

"Are you implying that I had something to do with your parents' death, Sheraton?" His dark brow furrowed in a deep line.

"No, sir..." *not implying—accusing.*

"To even think so is ludicrous. Lucas and Meredith were great friends. Losing them hurts me as much as it hurts you. How could you think otherwise?"

I leaned back, wishing I could get a better 'read' on him. I wasn't convinced, but I didn't want to cross the line any further. "I'm not, sir, not at all. Just...wondered... I appreciate your honesty, sir."

"You're welcome." Gordon smiled. "Now, are you ready to return to work? We have a lot on our plate and could use you."

I leaned forward. "Yes. I wanted to talk to you about the recent beheadings. I want to be put on that case."

Gordon looked out the window again, considering my request. "Strangest damn thing that's happened around here in a long time, for sure. Bobby's been working it day and night. Why do you want to be assigned to it?"

I didn't want to disclose anything about the supposed demon summoned to kill. Despite my relief at Gordon's apparent loyalty to the queen, I couldn't trust that he wasn't the one who summoned it, any more than I could trust that he had nothing to do with my parents 'death.'

"Has Bobby gotten anywhere with the case?"

Gordon shook his head. "No."

I shrugged, spreading my hands. "Then..."

"Yes. Good point. Okay, Blake. You take the lead but break it to Bobby gently, will you?"

"Yes sir, will do." I got up to leave, thankful the sweat pouring down my neck and back, soaking my shirt, was hidden under my warm jacket. Quickly stepping to the door, I grasped the handle, barely breathing. I couldn't wait to call Alex and tell her that Gordon believed my story and that I was on the case.

"Sheraton."

Dammit, moments from escape. "Yes, sir?"

"Welcome back."

"Thank you, sir." I stepped from the office and walked toward Bobby's desk.

CHAPTER
NINETEEN

ALEXANDRA

Magma had the patience of a saint. For all my sighing, hair pulling, and frustration—acting completely childish and losing patience—she somehow ignored me and forged on, reading through The Book.

I had nearly given up. We had been interpreting the damn thing for days. Blake was busy at work, figuring out who summoned the demon that murdered the witches.

Lucas and Meredith busied themselves helping Blake when they could, undercover, of course. They couldn't alert anyone to their existence. Not yet, anyway. At the moment, Meredith was curled up on the couch, engrossed in a selection of books from the library shelves. Lucas, high on the library ladder, creeping it from shelf to shelf, pouring over the volumes of 17th-century books, occasionally gasping at the collection.

Penny was busy with her life, and Teddy kept the Castle

Point Apothecary business—my business—running in my absence.

Carrigan had her businesses to run but promised to let us know if she had any ghostly visitors.

Everyone had their 'thing' to do. Mine was acting as secretary, note-taking Magma's interpretation. The Book itself was a piece of garbage, forged by the hand of the demon, Vine, for the benefit of Vine's 'commander' Earl Dagon.

It was no page-turner, that's for sure. It was as dry, dark, and evil as the Earl himself.

And mainly a lot of blah, blah, blah about how witches cursed the earth and need to be punished, stripped of their powers, and killed, and how the Witch Hunters—the dominant misogynistic lot of them—will reign.

I could thank myself and kick myself for that one.

As Evelyn of Cumbria incarnate, spurning Earl Dagon's love in the early 1600s and trying to escape his grasp resulted in the worst probable outcome for the witch population.

But I couldn't hold myself responsible forever.

I *could* find a way—*the* way—to end the Earl's reign from beyond the grave once and for all by ending the Witch Hunters.

For *that,* I could be a patient, willing secretary to the dear Crone who studiously poured over The Book. Magma broke my pity party.

"I think I found something!"

I nearly dropped my notes, scrambling to grasp them before they swept across the floor.

"What? What did you find, Magma?" My hands trembled. I placed my notes and pen on the desk and pulled up close. Meredith slammed the book she'd been reading shut and quickly came to Magma's side. Lucas quickly descended the library ladder and joined us.

"Here, see? These markings..."

I looked past the tip of her finger. In all honesty, the markings all looked the same to me. A bunch of squiggly, spermy-looking lines. The same gobbledygook I'd first laid eyes on the walls of Mitch Myles's cell and again on the scribbles my mother made at the sanatorium.

"What does it say? What do they mean?" Anticipation gurgled up from my belly into my throat and lodged there.

Magma took a deep breath. *"Should a witch defile a huntsman and elude the grasp of death, her powers may only be restored through the ancestral blood of a Dagon."*

"What does that mean?" Meredith asked, eyes wide as a full moon.

"Yes, exactly my question," I murmured. "Wait, does that mean what I think it means?"

"What do you think it means?" Magma asked, chuckling.

I blew out a breath. "Okay, yes, it's pretty self-explanatory. Earl Dagon made it impossible for a witch to regain her powers."

"How so?" Lucas asked.

"Well, how many witches did you know related to Earl Dagon? And how many ancestors of Earl Dagon would have been willing to help a witch—*if* she could have escaped a hunter's grasp?"

Lucas's eyebrow shot up. "Good point. None and no one."

"Exactly. But you do now."

"Who?" They asked in unison.

"Me."

"*You're* a Dagon ancestor?" Lucas asked.

"Yep. The last remaining, from what I'm told. Unless…"

"Unless what?" Again, in unison.

"Well, I never had the chance to talk to my mom about my ancestry. And I never knew my dad. His death has always been shrouded in mystery. I've always assumed *he* was my connection to Earl Dagon."

"But your father has passed…" Magma whispered.

"Yes, but what if I was wrong? What if it's my mom's side of the family?"

"Then you have a chance…" Lucas finished.

"Exactly. It's a fifty-fifty chance, but it's still a chance."

"How can you know for sure? It's not like you can ask your mother—she's under a curse."

"Yes, right? She's incoherent. We could try to lift the curse, but that's too risky."

"How so?" Meredith asked.

"Since losing my powers, I don't have…well, the power to lift the curse, and my previous attempts haven't been successful. And I refuse to put any other witches in danger, so I have asked no one from the underground to help."

"But we could help!" Meredith smiled.

"Thank you, but no. That would be ten times riskier. We can't let anyone see you or know you are alive—not yet, anyway."

"I'm confused," Meredith asked, tilting her head. "If we *can* help, but it's too risky, and you don't *want* our help… then what do you propose…?"

"I could summon the one person who may know. My mentor, Cressy. He may have kept that information from me and conveniently neglected to tell me I was the incarnation of Evelyn of Cumbria, but that was because he wanted to protect me from the truth. He might do the same in this case, as well."

The three nodded their heads, murmuring understanding,

"Let's do that, yes?" Lucas asked. "I'd enjoy seeing Waldo again. It's been some time…"

"Yes, let's. I'll need your help with the summoning part. Is that okay? I'm a limp horse without powers. Useless…"

"Of course, Alexandra, happy to help." Lucas patted me on the back, coaxing a smile from me.

"Okay, let's set up in the hall. It's too cold for the courtyard, and most rooms are closed off to keep the winter chill at bay."

For the next hour, we bustled around, preparing a space to summon Cressy. Blackjack did his part, as usual, surveying the assembly and pacing the circle, meowing in anticipation. My nerves were tight and on edge, so the occasional cuddle with Blackjack gave me peace.

As I moved around the hall, I wracked my brain, trying to remember my mom talking about my ancestry. How did I even come to know I'm the last remaining Dagon? I couldn't put a finger on it and got a headache trying.

Cressy, you better be able to shed a little light on my past. I whispered as I lit the last candle.

The smoke from the cauldron swirled in its usual fashion just before my friend and mentor appeared.

"Cressy," I breathed as his suave self appeared in the circle, wearing his usual deep purple suede smoking jacket, pencil-thin mustache, and eyes that held centuries of truth and myth.

"Your Grace," Cressy bowed slightly, grasping my hand with his translucent one, placing a feather-lite kiss on the back of my hand.

"For the love of the Goddess, Cressy. Stop that." I couldn't help but laugh.

Cressy's booming laughter filled the cavernous hall. "I'm so sorry, my dear. I couldn't help myself."

Shaking my head, grinning, I turned to my guests. "Cressy, this is Magma, and I believe you know…"

"Lucas and Meredith Sheraton! What a…surprise. Alexandra, does this mean you've found the handsome Mr. Sheraton?"

"Yes, Cressy. He showed up a few days ago, living and breathing, his living and breathing parents in tow." I smiled at the Sheraton's.

"Alexandra, I know you've been keeping company with a Witch Hunter, but now, his parents as well? A High Commander, no less. Who's death they blamed on a witch? Pray, young lady, what has happened to you? Rooting for the other side? Has the weight of your new crown tilted your viewpoint?" Cressy looked gobsmacked, his eyes wide, his mustachioed lip quivering in the candlelight.

I laughed despite myself. "No, Cressy. Not hunters. Witches. All of them. Even Blake."

Cressy eyed me, his brow furrowing into a deep line. "I'm sorry, my dear, but you're going to have to explain."

We explained.

When we finished, Cressy let out a low whistle. "This is just too fantastic a tale to believe."

"Isn't it, though? But it's all true". I spread my fingers wide and shrugged.

"So, have you summoned me to tell the tale, or was there something else I can assist with?"

My mouth went dry. "There *is* something…"

"Please, no more suspense, young lady. I've had quite enough for today. Ask, already."

I glanced at Lucas and Meredith, whose eyes urged me to continue. "Magma has found an interpretation in The

Book of the Order of the Witch Hunters. A spell that can bring a witch's power back once stripped."

"But that's incredible news, Alexandra. Well done, Magma!" Cressy nodded toward Magma, who smiled rather flirtatiously.

"Well, it is, and it isn't. See, it requires ancestral Dagon blood..."

Cressy's eyebrow shot up. "You know you're the last of that line..."

"Yes, but...Cressy, which side of the family does my blood run? If it's my mother's, we're good, but if it's my father's...I need to know for sure. I'd hate to draw blood from my mother unnecessarily."

Cressy slowly nodded, tapping a yellowing finger to his chin. "Good question, my dear."

"One you have the answer for, yes?" A seed of hope rooted inside me.

Cressy bowed his head, clasping his hands behind his transparent figure. I didn't need my witchy senses to know I wouldn't like what was coming next. "Your father was like you, Alexandra."

That was not what I wanted to hear.

"He was a witch, you mean?"

"He felt torn between two worlds, just like you are now. One foot in the witching world, one foot in the Dagon realm."

"He...he *wanted* to be a Dagon? He was...*proud* of it?"

"Yes, but he was also a witch. You inherited both your abilities from him, and he, from his father, and so on down the line to..." Cressy paused, looking at me woefully. His eyes turned down, creased at their edges.

"To...what, Cressy? Please, tell me." My hands shook by my side.

"To the child Earl Dagon had...with Evelyn of Cumbria."

The wind fell out of me, and I doubled over.

Meredith and Magma came to my side, steadying me.

"Waldo," Lucas asked, "there's no record of the Earl and Evelyn ever bearing a child. Can you be sure?"

Cressy nodded solemnly. "They did, indeed. Evelyn delivered shortly before Earl Dagon...destroyed her. He and his new bride, Madeline Bavant, raised the child as their own."

I cringed. "Th...that means...me, as Evelyn of Cumbria incarnate, I am...my ancestor?" Cressy slowly nodded. "And my father...he was also my...my what, exactly?"

Cressy's mouth worked as he licked his ghostly lips. "Evelyn is you and your father's grandmother from approximately twenty generations ago."

"Cress, why didn't you tell me this before? When I had asked you about Evelyn, and you told me I had been her in my past life?"

Cressy gave a slight shrug. "It wasn't pertinent. Also, your witchy powers were intact then."

I took a shaky breath. "Cressy. Are you sure that my father is not alive? That I am truly the last remaining ancestor of...Evelyn and the Earl?"

Cressy slowly nodded his head. "Yes, Alexandra. I'm afraid so."

Words came to my lips, but I couldn't ask. I took another shattered breath, steeling my nerves. "Cressy. I have to ask you something. Please be honest."

"Of course, my dear, please ask."

"How did my father die?"

"Of a broken heart, I believe."

"What do you mean?"

"Well, your mother and father were never married.

Having a child out of wedlock was frowned upon. When your mother found out she was pregnant with you, she knew exactly what that would mean. She would bear a witch and Dagon ancestor and couldn't bear to lose you to the pyre under Earl Dagon's rule, so she promised to keep you safe and your powers under wraps. She ended the affair and sent your father away, telling others they had married, but he died. It was a foreshadowing. For some weeks later, he was found dead, alone in his home, several counties away."

Sobs wracked my body. Meredith and Magma wrapped their arms around me. Lucas came closer, placing a warm hand on my back. It was several moments before I could speak again.

"I didn't know, Cressy. Any of it."

Cressy stepped back, eyes wide. "You didn't know...the truth about your parents?"

I nodded, wiping my nose with my sweater sleeve. "Yes. I had asked my mother a few times, but she just said he died and never to ask again. There were no pictures of my father anywhere, and none of their wedding. I guess I just assumed..."

"Of course, sweetheart. An understandable assumption to make, based on the circumstances." Meredith said as Magma pulled a clean tissue from the sleeve of her sweater and handed it to me.

"My mother. She was so hard on me as a child. She would p...p...punish me for using my powers..."

"I know, sweet girl. It's taken you a long time to overcome the pain of it all. I'm so sorry, Alexandra, not just for the pain of revealing the truth but for being unable to offer you an ancestry to draw blood from."

Fresh tears spilled onto my cheeks. I couldn't speak.

Magma stepped toward Cressy. "It's okay, Waldo. We will find another way. I haven't finished my interpretation of The Book yet. There is still hope."

"Please, if I can further assist, call on me. Alexandra, I'm so sorry. I hope you can forgive me for delivering such terrible news." Cressy enveloped me in a cold hug as I stared into space, and Cressy faded.

When he was gone, I saw a movement from my periphery. I glanced down the hall in time to see a tall, stoic figure —Malcolm—disappear into the shadows.

CHAPTER
TWENTY

BLAKE

Bobby and I had been poring over the details of two beheadings. So far, nothing Bobby had turned up was of much use. We were no closer to figuring out who summoned the demon Murder than Alexandra was to finding a spell to return her powers.

A few evenings back, after work, I had gone to my apartment before going to Castle Dagon—under cover of darkness, in case anyone was to follow me and know I was canoodling with the new queen—only to find the queen absolutely shattered. She had summoned her mentor and discovered a few things about her family she hadn't counted on. I stayed and held her while she cried on my shoulder, pouring out the entire story. Once I was sure Alex was calm, I tucked her in, returned to my place, poured a Bourbon, and processed everything she told me while keeping my emotions intact.

As much as I wanted to take our relationship to the next level, now was not the time.

But try telling 'little Blake' that.

Whenever I got close to Alex, no matter her emotional condition, I wanted to be...even closer. So, until it was right, little Blake and big Blake slept at home, joining Alex and my family for late dinners or early breakfasts.

"Here's the updated list of potential suspects, Blake." Bobby handed me a printout. I read over the names briefly, mentally noting which of those were Witch Hunters and who were not. I couldn't let Bobby—a 'fellow' Witch Hunter—know that the men killed were witches. Therefore, all Witch Hunters were at the top of every list in my books.

"Okay, great, Bob. Can you follow up with these, get their alibis, and let me know?"

"Sure, will do, boss. Hey, are you attending the conclave next week?"

I hoped my face wasn't showing my disgust. "Uh, yeah. I guess."

"It should be a good one. What's your position on this whole queen thing, anyway?"

I peered at him from across the desk. "Earl Dagon named Alexandra Heale queen Bob. His rules are our rules. End of story. You have a problem with that?" Bobby quickly became one hunter on my 'watch' list.

"Yeah, no, of course not. Rules are rules."

I was about to proceed with a lecture but got distracted by a burst of activity in the bullpen and a harsh knock on my door.

"Come in." I stood up.

The door burst open, and Jeffrey Deibert walked in. His large frame, blue suit, bolo tie, and white stetson made him larger and louder than life. "Hey Sheraton, you're back! I heard you got lost in the woods. You were out camping and forgot your compass?" Jeff reached out to shake my hand, but remembering that he had stolen Penny's powers of psychic insight, I didn't want him touching me and figuring out my true identity. I ignored his hand, reached for my coffee cup, and refilled it from the carafe on my desk.

"Jeff. Good to..." I couldn't finish my sentence. It was *never* good to see Jeff Deibert, so why would I say it? "Have you met Deputy Bobby?" Jeff grabbed Bobby's hand.

"What can we do for you, Mayor?" Bobby asked.

Jeff turned to me. "Well, I just wanted to ensure there were no hard feelings about that whole Penny business. I acted on it faster than you could, so I still feel justified..."

Darkness crept up my spine. My witch senses were on full alert. I wanted this guy gone. "Sure, Jeff. No hard feelings. Don't mention it."

"Well, you disappeared the night of the ceremony. I assumed you were just pissed and took off, acting like a child having a tantrum. Good to know you were just 'lost'." A devious grin etched Jeff's features. His dark eyes went even darker. "Besides, I didn't get the chance to finish her and burn her on the pyre. So, you can sleep at night knowing she's still livin' and breathin'. Her powers, however, have given me an edge. Too bad you didn't act on that when you should have. Snooze, you lose as they say..."

His voice grated on my nerves. I studied his annoying smirk, lifting my eyebrow as high as possible, giving him my best non-impressed look. There was something definitely off about this guy. I decided I wanted to revisit the idea that Jeff was the one who summoned the demon Murder.

"Hey Jeff, don't change the subject. I mean, as much as I enjoy the recant of your...whatever." Jeff chuckled. I continued. "Have you heard anything about the recent murders?"

"Oh, sure, sure. Hasn't everyone? The weirdest thing.

Both those men were stand-up citizens of Castle Point. Damn shame. What do you boys make of it?" he addressed Bobby, who nodded toward me.

"Deputy Sheriff Sheraton is on the case, sir, so I'm sure we'll solve it soon." Bobby smiled.

Jeff guffawed. "Yeah, well. I guess we'll see about that. Anyhoo, I guess I should be going. I just wanted to..."

"Where were you the nights of the murders, Jeff?" I interrupted.

He studied me, his smile fading. "Why are you asking, Blake? I'm not a suspect."

"Everyone's a suspect, Jeff. You included. Answer the question, please."

Bobby's head lobbed from me to Jeff and back again. Eyes wide, he stayed quiet and watched the show.

Jeff stepped back and tipped his hat further on his head. "Well, I was at home, of course. Like every night."

"Do you have any proof of that?"

"I don't need proof, Sheraton. I'm the Mayor, for chrissakes."

"Doesn't mean you can't be a murderer. What's your alibi?"

Jeff blew a frustrated breath. "I didn't come here to be questioned about something I didn't do, Blake. And I take offense to the thought that I had anything to do with those murders."

I ignored him and pushed on. "You knew both the victims, didn't you?"

"Well, sure I did. As does everyone, Blake. It's a small town. What kind of policing have I hired you to do, anyway? You're wasting my time, precious money, and resources barking up the wrong tree!" he grabbed the door handle and pulled.

"Hey, Jeff...?"

"What?" he barked.

"Don't leave town."

He threw me a look and stomped out the door, slamming it behind him.

TWENTY-ONE

ALEXANDRA

I t felt like I'd slept for days.

The emotional rollercoaster of the past several weeks, topped off with Cressy's news about my ancestry, completely exhausted me.

And we were still no further in finding an alternate spell to reinstate my powers or finding whoever summoned the demon to stop it.

If it weren't for seeing Blake twice a day when he had the time, I wouldn't even bother brushing my teeth or putting on anything other than sweats. On the days when he wasn't coming over for breakfast, I could sleep in and give absolutely zero farts.

"Dear Goddess, woman. Snap out of it. Your self-indulgent pity party is getting old." Blackjack sat on my pillow beside my head, his tail flicking my face.

"Blackjack, go away. Leave me to wallow in peace." I turned my face toward him to avoid his insistent tail snapping and was abruptly rewarded with a back-end blast from his kitty ass. "Eww, Blackjack! Go!" I hurled myself and Blackjack from the bed.

"Got you up though, didn't I?" he snarked, walking out the door, tail high. *"See you downstairs for breakfast,* your Highness."

I sighed and resignedly got into the shower.

I headed down the hall toward the kitchen when I was clean, dry, and dressed. I wasn't hungry for food, but I was for Blake's company.

And coffee. Vats of coffee.

Teddy rushed up the stairs of my wing and toward me. "Alex, we need to talk."

I halted. "Of course, Ted. Sorry, I've been so out of it lately. Is it the store? Is everything okay?"

"Yes, just super-fantabulous, of course. Sales have been up since you took the throne."

I forced a smile. "Well, there's at least one perk to wearing this crown." I pointed to the imaginary crown on top of my head. "Is that what you came to tell me?"

Teddy shook her pigtails, glamored a cheery pink today. "No, it's Malcolm."

That stopped me short. Malcolm had witnessed my conversation with Cressy the night we summoned him, or at least part of it. I hadn't spoken to him since. "What about Malcolm?"

"Late last night, long after you'd gone to bed, I left my herbal room—I'd been up most of the night working on new potions to get your powers back—and saw Malcolm open a secret door that led to a passageway within the walls of the castle."

"What? Where?"

"Under the stairs."

Cold chills swiftly burst through me. To me, 'under the

stairs' held a dark meaning. When I played with my powers as a child, my mother would lock me in a hidden closet under the stairs of the house I grew up in. When I was a child, I didn't know it was because she was trying to protect me from the Witch Hunters, but I swore never to enter a dark space again.

"Do you know what he was doing under there?"

Teddy dropped her voice to a whisper and looked behind her. "I followed him."

"You what? Oh, Teddy, that's so dangerous. Did you take the hounds with you, at least?"

"No. I know I took a chance, but I just had to find out where he went."

I could barely breathe. "And...? Did you? What did you see?"

"The tunnel, it led to a...chamber type-thing. I saw Malcolm performing a ritual. With candles and some weird animal skulls and incense...everything. He was chanting, or maybe it was praying, but he was talking to...something...in some weirdo funky language."

Another chill flew through me. "Did it sound like the Witch Hunter language, Latin, or the old Wiccan?"

Teddy shrugged. "I don't know...could have been any of those? I'm no expert. Sorry, Alex."

"Don't be sorry, Teddy. Thank you for bringing this to my attention."

"Of course. Seems like Creepster McGee has some super spooky habits we don't know about."

"Yes, it would seem that way." We walked to the kitchen together. Meredith, Lucas, Magma, and Blake were already chatting around the breakfast table. Malcolm was serving everyone. When he returned to the counter to reload his tray, I motioned for him to chat.

"Yes, your Grace? What is it you require?"

"I'd think you and I need to talk, Malcolm. Not now, but when we have a chance, this afternoon, perhaps?"

"Of course, your Grace. Can I ask...what this is concerning? Have I not managed the castle well enough for you?"

"You've done a fine job, Malcolm. It's...something else. Meet me at the library early this afternoon."

"Yes, your Grace." Malcolm proceeded with serving breakfast. I sat at the table across from Teddy, whose eyes flicked from me to Malcolm and back again. I gave a small smile and gestured an okay symbol.

After breakfast, Blake left for the station, and the rest of us took up our usual positions. Magma and I were reading The Book, Lucas and Meredith went through lists of Witch Hunter suspects, and Teddy left to open the Apothecary.

I must have checked my watch a thousand times. The closer it got to the afternoon, the more tense I became. I kept going over what I'd say to Malcolm. I decided the direct approach was best. Let him know I saw him slip into the secret passageway—I didn't want to mention Teddy's involvement—and then ask him what ritual he was performing and why.

My nerves frayed thinking about him being the one who summoned and was in control of the demon. Meeting him while I was powerless was utterly insane. I regretted not telling Blake my plans.

"Alexandra, dear. What troubles have you so distracted today?" Magma asked. I realized I had missed transcribing about two pages of Magma's interpretation.

"I'm so sorry, Magma. I have to meet with Malcolm to discuss...well, discuss his potentially being the one who summoned the demon that committed the murders."

Lucas overheard. "Alexandra, what's this? You suspect Malcolm, your butler?"

I nodded and filled them in on the details Teddy shared with me that morning.

Meredith shook her head. "You can't possibly meet with him on your own, Alexandra. What if your suspicions are correct? No, you need us and our powers."

"Meredith, I wouldn't ask you to..."

"Enough of that, Alexandra," Lucas interrupted. "You aren't asking. We are insisting. If Malcolm is dangerous, you need our magic to back you up."

I nodded resignedly. A warm heat flowed through my chilly nerves. I didn't feel so alone for the first time in a long while. "Okay, fine. Please stay. He should have been here a while ago. I told him to meet me in the library early this afternoon. It's already mid-afternoon now." I walked to the gold-braided rope and pulled. Pacing, the four of us twiddled our thumbs and picked invisible lint off our clothes, waiting for Malcolm to show. When he did not, I pulled the braided rope again, then walked into the hallway and called his name.

No answer.

"Let's split up and look for him." Lucas offered.

We went our separate ways, leaving Magma in the library if he showed up. Searching everywhere and asking the other staff, Malcolm was nowhere to be found. When we met again a few minutes later, I led Lucas and Meredith to the staircase.

"Teddy said she saw him enter a passageway somewhere around...here..." The three of us slid our hands across the castle rockwork until I finally found a loose stone and pulled. A stone doorway opened inward. The hallway inside was dimly lit, with a few small torches. Lucas and I walked into the tunnel. The air smelled dank and dusty, but the floor and walls were dry.

"I'll stay behind to ensure no one closes the door on you two," Meredith offered.

We walked softly, mindful of the echo of footsteps down the tunnel. Dusting away the cobwebs as we walked, we came across the vestibule Teddy had seen Malcolm enter. Inside was a small table with incense, candles, and other items rarely found on a witch's altar.

"Do any of these things look like they're part of a Witch Hunter ritual?"

Lucas shook his head, turning over several small animal skulls. "No. Not at all. Perhaps Wiccan, but...they seem a little darker in purpose. Voodoo, perhaps?"

I shrugged. "I couldn't tell you, but I have a feeling this has much more to do with summoning the demon than I first expected."

Lucas took out his iPhone and took several pictures before we placed the items back where we saw them and retreated from the space.

Once we emerged from the tunnel and replaced the stone, closing the door, I told Lucas and Meredith to meet me back at the library.

I had a call to make.

Heading to Mr. Fellows's old office, now Teddy's herbal kitchen, I picked up the phone and called Mr. Fellows at home. He answered on the third ring.

"Ello?"

"Mr. Fellows, hello. It's Alexandra. Alexandra Heale."

"Oh, hello, Alexandra! How lovely to hear from you! To what do I owe this call?"

"Well, I wanted to talk to you about Malcolm."

"Malcolm?"

"Yes. We discussed him at length when I called for references, but I was hoping..."

"Alexandra, I'm sorry, my dear. I know my memory isn't quite what it used to be, but I can't put a finger on conversing with you about a fellow named Malcolm..."

I swallowed hard. "Oh, sure you do. Malcolm. Tall, strange-looking man. He looks a little like Lurch from the Addams Family. He used to be your 'right-hand man' when you were curator at the castle museum..." *Please remember him, please remember him, please remember him...*

"I'm sorry, Alexandra, but in the thirty years that I was curator of the Castle Dagon museum, I never had an employee named Malcolm at my right hand or otherwise..."

Blood rushed to my head, and I dropped the phone.

CHAPTER
TWENTY-TWO

BLAKE

I rushed back to the castle the minute Dad called. Alexandra had fainted, but that was all Dad would tell me over the phone. I knew it wasn't because she was pregnant. As much as I wanted to go there, we hadn't. So, unless it was immaculate conception, it was something else. It was likely just pure exhaustion.

Alexandra and I spent our time together sorting through the case files of the murder while Magma continued her interpretation of The Book. Although I'd rather be doing anything else with Alex, I craved our time together, whatever the reason. At least we had Lucas and Meredith as the buffer between us, or perhaps this fainting spell would have been because she was carrying my child.

A warm heat flooded through me at the thought. I had thought about Alex and me as a permanent item several times but never considered having children with her.

My body's reaction surprised me.

When I arrived at the castle and rushed to the library,

Alexandra was conscious, lying on the couch, my mother tending to her.

"What happened?" I asked, vying for space on the couch beside Alex. She sat up but felt woozy.

Dad spoke up. "Alexandra suspects Malcolm is the one who summoned the demon. When she requested a meeting with him, he disappeared."

"What? How did you come to think he's the one?"

"Teddy saw him head into a secret passageway under the stairs. We found the tunnel and followed it to a small altar room." Dad showed me the pictures of the items on the altar.

"Weird. But then again, so is Malcolm. Did either of you sense he was dangerous?" I nodded toward my parents, but they shook their heads.

"Not in the slightest, just a bit strange."

"Well, I'm suspicious, especially since he disappeared," Alex said, rubbing the back of her head. "I called Mr. Fellows, the old museum curator, who gave me a glowing reference about Malcolm. Turns out, he's never heard of the man and never had him in his employ."

"What? But you'd spoken to him about Malcolm before hiring him?"

"Yes, at least, I thought it was Mr. Fellows I was speaking with. It wasn't."

"So, you're telling me that Malcolm somehow installed himself in the castle as your butler, for...what reason?"

"That's what we don't know. But we assume he's the one who summoned the demon to kill the witches..." Mom said.

I shook my head. "Just because you have a weird altar table doesn't mean he's Murder's commander. But it also doesn't mean you should trust him. That he disappeared is highly suspicious."

"Agreed," Dad said. "I think we need to up the security around here until we know more."

"Yes. I'll pack a bag."

"You'll what?" Alex eyed me.

"I'm moving in."

Alex smiled.

My heart flipped.

"What do we do to find Malcolm? Have you made any headway in finding the demon?" she asked.

"We could try scrying for him. And no, we aren't getting anywhere with the inquiry into the murders. We need to figure out how to flush out the demon or the person who summoned it." I said.

"The only thing we know is it could be anyone," Lucas said.

Alex piped up, "What if we started with the Witch Hunters? I could call a meeting, insist they all gather here."

"And do what, exactly?" I asked.

Alex shrugged. "I don't know..."

Dad piped up. "I think I know. Meredith and I could show ourselves. Tell them we didn't die. Tell them we are witches."

I slammed a hand against the coffee table, ruffling the files they had poured over. "What good would that do other than put you in danger? We still don't know who tried to kill you and Mom."

Mom agreed. "Lucas, that could be suicide. Why would you even suggest it?"

Lucas spread his hands. "two birds with one stone, perhaps? The bait and switch approach?"

"I'm confused." Alex said, "You think that by baiting the

hunters with...well, you...that it would flush out your potential killer *and* the person who's summoned the demon?"

"Precisely."

Alex and I looked at each other.

"Worth a shot, I suppose," I said.

Alex agreed. "It's the best idea we've had yet. The only idea. Okay, I'll make the call." A little unsteadily, Alex walked to the desk, picked up the phone, and called Sheriff Roberts—High Commander. "Okay, he set the local Witch Hunters meeting for tonight." She sat back on the couch. Because the murders occurred locally, we had to assume that if a hunter had summoned the demon, that hunter was also local. It was as good a place to start as any.

"Great. We expose ourselves as alive-and-well witches in a few hours and flush out a murderer." Dad seemed pretty confident.

"Or," I injected, "We have a massive battle on our hands."

"Always the Negative Nancy." Alex teased, ruffling my hair.

"Not negative, just...realistic in my expectations." I grinned, pulling her closer to me.

"Okay, you two. Keep it in your pants. We have a meeting to prepare for."

"Dad!"

I looked at Alex. She was thirty shades of blush, but her sly smile told me 'it' was on her mind...

We prepared the large dining room for the hunter's meeting. The courtyard was larger and could hold more people standing in a circle, but this wasn't a night for a ritual.

It was a night for a revelation.

Besides, the fresh snowfall, chilly temperatures, and Alex's nailing the courtyard doors shut made the decision easy.

Also, the new law. No witch-hunter meetings were sanctioned since Alex's rise to the throne. She had made it illegal. So, tonight was just a meeting. No robes, no ritual, just hunters.

We stoked the giant fireplace in the dining hall until it was blazing. Teddy came home from the shop, and she and Alex prepared mulled wine and snacks, which I found amusing.

"You trying to make friends, Alex?" I teased.

She gave me a look. "Yes, I am. I probably should have done this months ago when the Earl gave me the title."

"What? Hold an open invitation for the hunters to mingle with their new queen? The peasants are revolting, your Majesty. Or had you forgotten that you're not so loved worldwide?"

She gave me a look. "There you go, being all 'Negative Nancy' again. Or perhaps, 'Blasphemous Blake'? I'm sure I could handle a bunch of idiot hunters."

I shot her a look back. "Might I remind you, I used to *be* one of those idiots? Plus, I'm the one with the powers here."

"Hey! Low blow, Sheraton. Low blow," she pouted.

Laughing, I pulled her into a quick hug. "Sorry, Alex. I couldn't resist. Let me help you with the wine and snacks. But first..." I grabbed a mug and scooped up some of the mulled wine for a taste. Alex knocked the mug out of my hand.

"Hey!"

"Sorry, but Teddy spiked the wine."

"Spiked it? With what? More wine? Are you hoping to get the hunters drunk? Take advantage of them?"

"No, silly. We're hoping to extract the truth."

"You mean…"

"Yuperdoodle!" Teddy shouted, then lowered her voice. "We spiked it with a truth serum."

"Ahh, clever." I slowly clapped my approval.

Teddy tapped herself on the head. "Not just a head full of colorful hair and pigtails, my friend."

I grabbed Alex around the waist. "Whose idea was that? Yours?"

"Of course. But Teddy's brilliance created the potion."

Teddy beamed as she scooped the concoction into large carafes to keep it hot.

"And you didn't want me to tell you any truths?" I asked.

Alex laughed. "I assume you do that already. Was I wrong?"

I shook my head. "What's in the snacks? More witchy wonders?"

Alex laughed. "No, those I made."

"Ahh, nice. She's not only gorgeous, she can cook, too." I grabbed a chocolate square and popped it in my mouth before Alex could bat it away.

We piled the plates of goodies and carafes of wine onto trays and carried them to the dining hall, Teddy's hounds following close behind. Mom and Dad were there, arranging chairs.

"Oh, nice. I could use some wine." Lucas grabbed a cup.

"No!" we shouted, taking Dad entirely by surprise. Laughing, I explained.

"Oh, well, that's quite brilliant." Dad smiled.

Mom added, "You will have to serve everyone the wine as they come in, before asking them questions, and, of course, before Lucas and I make our appearance."

Alex and I agreed. Teddy spoke up. "I'm going to handle that. We can't have the Queen of the Witch Hunters lifting a finger." She swooped her hands over her body, and an adorable maid's uniform appeared.

"Cute, Teddy, thank you." Alex smiled, fluttering her hand to her earring.

"You nervous, Alex?" I asked.

She nodded. "Extremely."

I pulled her hand away from her earring and held it. "Hey, you have us here to back you up. Don't forget that."

She nodded and smiled up at me. "Right, yes, of course, thank you. Teddy, can you ask another staff to manage the door? Have the hounds there to greet everyone as well. Not glamored, but...natural."

"Good idea, boss. Doin' it! Come on, boys. But you have to promise to be good. No snacking on hunters unless mommy says it's okay." The hounds barked—more like snarled—their agreement. Teddy scampered off the hounds at her heels.

"Where's Magma?" Alex asked.

Mom answered. "She shuffled off to bed. Told us to yell if her powers were required." She laughed. "She said her head was full of Witch Hunter lore, and if she had to spend one more minute in the presence of anything relating to it, she couldn't be responsible for what she would do."

A loud knock came from the massive iron door knocker on the front door.

The first hunter to arrive was Sheriff Roberts and Jeff Deibert. I shook their hands and pretended I had arrived just minutes before them. Alex was amiable, but I could tell she was nervous. I wanted to reach out and touch her, place my hand on the base of her spine to steady her, but I thought better of it. I'd already told Gordon we weren't involved and didn't want to jeopardize either relationship.

As other hunters arrived, Teddy offered everyone a small mug of wine and snacks. I watched each hunter's face, looking for signs of trouble but also looking for signs of the potion taking effect. I saw none, so I assumed it would work when the time was right.

"Well, your Grace, to what do we owe the honor of this meeting?" Gordon's voice boomed above the din, instantly hushing the sizeable crowd of hunter-locals. The gathering was not vast, and many of the guys not in attendance were on-duty officers.

Alex stood on the fireplace's hearth, placing her slightly higher than the crowd, and cleared her throat. "I have a question for you all." A torrent of whispers flowed through the room. Alex ignored them and continued clearing her throat again. "Who among you summoned the demon, Murder?"

The entire room went as silent as a broken vacuum.

"Your Grace?" Gordon spoke. "I'm not sure what you're asking. There's a demon in Castle Point?"

Alex nodded. "Yes. A demon is, in fact, the one who committed the recent murders. A demon *named* Murder." Another ripple of whispers and surprise rumbled across the room. "Am I to assume that none of you summoned the demon who's committed these crimes?"

"Your *Majesty*," Jeff Deibert piped up, his tone snarky. "What exactly makes you think a demon is involved? And, better yet, that a Witch Hunter summoned said demon?"

"I have it on good authority...and..."

"Oh, good *authority*. I see. Well, as a Witch Hunter and a citizen of Castle Point, I can tell you I take offense to the ridiculous notion." Jeff boomed, hands firmly on his hips. The hunters around the room spoke their protests.

Alexandra glanced over at me. I could see the fear in her eyes. Some hunters started laughing, and others left.

This was quickly becoming a shit show.

I jumped up on the hearth beside Alex and whistled. "Hey, everyone, get back here, settle down and listen. Alexandra is telling the truth. And she asked you all a question. Which of you—or have any of you—summoned the demon known as 'Murder'?"

The crowd fell silent, each hunter looking from one to another and around the room.

Shit. Nobody's raising a hand. Either the summoner isn't here, or the potion didn't work.

I took the next step. "Well, if you aren't willing to come forward and admit it to your queen, perhaps you will to your High Commander."

Gordon, brow wrinkled, looked up at me. "Blake, what are you doing? I'm not asking..."

"Not you, Gordon. The *real* High Commander of the Order."

"Blake, what are you talking about? I *am* the real High Commander."

At that moment, my parents entered the room.

TWENTY-THREE

ALEXANDRA

"You can't be High Commander if your predecessor is still alive." Blake grinned and addressed Gordon.

"Blake, what the…"

Lucas and Meredith walked into the room and joined us on the hearth.

Gasps from the oldest members of the local Order flooded the room like a foghorn on a lighthouse. The younger members whispered questions and uttered gasps of disbelief when those questions were answered.

Gordon and Jeffrey both stood stock still, mouths gaping.

"Hello, Gordon. Nice to see you again," Lucas said rather calmly.

Gordon sputtered, "L…Lucas. Meredith! What? How…?"

"You mean you didn't know that we were alive? And have been, all along?"

Gordon slowly shook his head, his eyes never leaving

Lucas's. "N...no. I thought you'd died. I saw you...buried you..."

"You saw nothing and buried a couple of empty coffins."

"But why?"

Lucas stepped off the hearth to stand directly in front of Gordon. "You mean you really don't know, Gordon? You don't know why we had to fake our deaths and leave our son behind?"

Gordon merely shook his head.

Lucas continued, "Because our lives were being threatened, Gordon. By someone close to us."

"What? Why? And Who?"

"The who is what we were hoping you could tell us," Blake began, "The why is because..." he looked to both his parents, who nodded their support. "Because we're witches."

The hushed murmurs that had rippled through the crowd of hunters turned to a thunderous roar. The angry fervor transported me back to the courtyard, about to lose my powers and burn on the pyre. Hunters left, right, and center were jeering, throwing insults, and daring the witches to show them 'what you got.'

Things were teetering on being out of control. I wanted to shrink into the background.

Then Blake took over, and everything shifted.

"Everyone shut the hell up!" He yelled. The crowd calmed somewhat. "I'm going to remind you we all have a new queen, whether we are hunters or not. And we are all obligated to follow the queen's rule, whether we like it or not. Anyone who disobeys that rule will have to answer to me directly." Then Blake did something I hadn't expected or seen him do since returning to Castle Point.

He opened his palm and raised a glowing, bright energy ball.

"Am I understood?" He cupped his free hand to his ear. A quiet, submissive response came from the crowd. "I asked, AM I UNDERSTOOD?" That earned a much louder response. "Good." He closed his palm, looked at me, and winked.

I nearly orgasmed on the spot.

I mean, Blake as Blake is incredible. Blake *with powers*...?

Absofuckinglutely amazing.

I'll have to ask him to do that again later.

Right now, I needed to peel my eyes off of him and focus.

Lucas spoke. "Does anyone here know who it was that threatened our lives so many years ago?

The crowd murmured in hushed denial. Lucas took a deep breath. "Gordon? I'm asking you directly. Did you have anything to do with the threat to our lives?"

Gordon merely shook his head. "No, Lucas. You were my friend. Honestly, I'm insulted that you didn't trust me with..."

"With what, Gordon? My secret? Did you honestly expect me to confess to being a witch...to a hunter? Even one who was supposedly my 'closest friend'?"

"How could you be a witch and a High Commander? Who was lying to whom, Lucas?" Gordon spat.

Lucas looked down, then at his wife. Taking his hand, Meredith urged him on. He looked Gordon in the eyes once again. "I did lie to you, yes. But I couldn't exactly admit that I was infiltrating the Order now, could I?"

Jeffrey Deibert's voice boomed. "You smug son-of-a-bitch. You ought to be hung!" Many of the crowd vehemently agreed.

Blake, Lucas, and Meredith raised their hands and activated energy balls. Teddy, who was only steps away, followed suit. The hounds started a low growl. The dining room hushed, everyone moving back, further away from the witches and the hounds.

And I am the magic-less queen, smack-dab in the middle.

I wanted to laugh.

I stepped off the hearth and closer to the hunters.

"Alex..." Blake warned. I waved him off.

Conjuring my best regal voice, I commanded them all to stop. "Enough, already. I know most of you don't recognize my authority here, but I think you can all agree that if you want a battle, we will come, fireballs blazing." I pointed to the witches behind me. "I can only count one or two of you in this group that *has* any powers—ones you stripped from a witch, no less," I fixed my hands on my hips and stared at Jeff Deibert, whose smug smile I wanted to wipe off his face. "So, consider this a warning. Please don't mess with me or my family of witches. ANY witches. The Witch Hunters are done. Over. Finito. We have a much bigger issue on our hands. Finding a demon, or the person who summoned it, and stopping him. You hear me?"

Many of the hunters nodded. Others shook their heads in contempt.

"Good. So, let me ask you again. Who here is responsible for conjuring the demon, Murder?"

Again, nothing. I looked at Teddy, who lifted her shoulders in a high shrug.

The potion must not be working. Or we're barking at the wrong crowd.

"Okay, fine, be that way." I continued. "Whoever is interested in helping us find the demon, stay. The rest of you...dismissed."

Everyone left.

Except for Gordon Roberts.

"Your Grace, you have my—and my office's—full support."

"Sheriff, the officers who attended the meeting all left." I pointed out.

"And they will be reprimanded, I can assure you. I will put every officer in Castle Point on this case, like it or not."

He offered his hand, and I shook it. "Thank you, Sheriff."

Gordon looked from Lucas to Meredith and back again. "I'd also appreciate spending time with my old friends."

Lucas's eyes creased with a smile. "I'd appreciate that also, Gordon."

"It's good to see you again, Gordon," Meredith added.

Blake stepped off the hearth and slid his arm around me. I looked up at him, surprised, as did Gordon. Blake didn't seem to care. "It's late, and her Grace needs her beauty sleep."

"Hey! I'm a big girl. I decide on my bedtime. Thank you very much."

Blake laughed. "Let's agree to reconvene tomorrow and make a plan, okay?

Everyone agreed.

Lucas and Meredith walked Gordon to the door and said goodnight.

Teddy, Blake, and I cleared up the mugs and carafes of mulled wine. Teddy took the first tray to the kitchen.

"Looks like the potion didn't work," Blake said, pouring the last of one carafe into a mug and swallowing it down. "Or, if it did work, then the hunters had nothing to do with either summoning the demon or attempting to kill my parents."

"Which is crappy," I agreed, "because, now, Lucas and Meredith have exposed themselves as living, breathing witches for nothing."

"Zackly," Blake slurred. "Okay, I finished the wine. Go ahead, test me. Ask me anything."

Hmm, this could be fun.

"Okay...tell me the truth, Mr. Sheraton. Do you know who summoned the demon?"

Blake looked at me, a big smile etched on his face.

"Yep."

TWENTY-FOUR

BLAKE

"You do?" Alex asked. She looked at me kinda funny.

"Do what?"

"Know who summoned the demon?"

"Oh. Yes." I said. Although I'm not sure why.

"For Goddess' sake Blake. Tell me!"

The room went a little fuzzy.

Did I know?

Wait, I think I did.

Yes, I did!

I looked at Alexandra with the straightest face I could muster. "Malcolm."

Why is she rolling her eyes at me?

"Blake, snap out of it!"

"Sorry. I dunno what's wrong with me. I feel a little... drunk."

Alexandra took the mug from my hand and sniffed it, then licked up what little wine there was. I felt all warm and lusty, watching her tongue as it flicked out and rimmed the mug. I licked my lips.

"Looks like Teddy's potion worked. You're feeling the effects of it. Do you assume Malcolm is the one who summoned the demon, or do you know for sure?"

"Yes."

"Yes, to which one, Blake?"

I had to think hard. "What was the question?"

Alex let out a huff and put her hand on her forehead. "Blake. Try to focus. Do you know for sure that Malcolm is the one who summoned the demon?"

I squinted at her, scrunching up my face, thinking hard. *Why did I think Malcolm was the one? Because he's weird, tall, and...weird.* That didn't seem like a reasonable answer. "Because...nobody else at this meeting said they did it, even after drinking the spiked wine. It makes the most sense."

Yeah, that sounded good.

"Hmm, I guess so. The problem is, what are we going to do about it?"

"Do about what?" Teddy asked as she walked into the dining hall to finish the cleanup.

"Teddy, it looks like your potion worked. Blake tried it, and now he's being goofy. Not sure why the Witch Hunters didn't all react like this when they drank it."

"He's goofier than usual? Maybe the potion affects witches differently?" Teddy giggled. "Did you ask him any super serious questions? Like, 'Do you looooove me?'..." Teddy clasped her hands under her chin and fluttered her eyelashes.

"No," I answered. I don't love you, I love Alexandra." *Whoa.* "Sorry, was that out loud?" I stared at their shocked faces.

"Okay, Sheraton. It's time to get some coffee for you. We

have work to do." Alex pulled me out of the room toward the kitchen.

Teddy just stood there, staring and grinning like a weirdo. "Oooo, glossing over the 'love' comment and changing the subject. Classic diversion tactic. Well done, boss."

"What work do we have to do?" I asked.

"Well, it's going to be hard to arrest Malcolm and stop the demon if we can't *find* Malcolm, so we have to scry for him. See if we can find his location."

When we got to the kitchen, Mom and Dad were there, tidying up. Alex brewed a couple of shots of espresso for me. While I sucked them back, she and Teddy grabbed a map of Dagon County, candles, a Spirit Board, and a pendulum. They spread the map on the kitchen table, and then all five of us stood around it. When they finished setting up, I felt much more like myself. With a dash of embarrassment heating my cheeks, I stood beside Alex.

"May I?" my mother asked, reaching for the pendulum.

"By all means," Alex said, smiling.

Mom held the pendulum over the map and chanted: "*Goddess good, Goddess great, be with us now to help locate. Malcolm is the one to find, so swing the pendulum divine.*"

Almost instantly, it swung wide, circling the map as Mom moved her hand in different directions, watching as the pendulum honed in on one area. Magma was teaching me location spells, but I hadn't had the chance to use one yet, so this was pretty cool.

"Look! It's swinging over our neighborhood." Teddy pointed.

Alex gasped. "He must be close."

"Uhh, Alex..." I pointed as the pendulum swung tighter

and tighter until it went ramrod straight—over the castle. "He's here."

Alex grabbed my arm. "Oh, my Goddess," she breathed.

"Blake, let's check the door." Dad bolted from the kitchen. We followed.

"He could be anywhere inside the castle," Alex said. "Teddy, maybe we should check the secret tunnel."

"Absolutely not!" Dad stopped short and spun around. "Not alone...he—"

"Dad!"

"Lucas!"

"Oh, no!"

The cacophony of yelling was quickly silenced when we realized the trouble Dad was in.

He stood there, facing us, his head locked in place as if held by an invisible hand, a large blade to his throat.

Nothing, or no one, was behind him, holding it.

The demon is here.

Dad is next.

Teddy's hellhounds immediately snarled, circling Dad. My cop instincts overrode the fear that flushed through me. "Dad, don't move," I instructed, flicking my hand open, an energy ball popping into my palm. Mom and Teddy did the same. I raised my voice. "You don't stand a chance, whatever or whoever you are. You're outnumbered. Get the blade away from my father's neck. Now."

A booming laugh filled the room, startling us all. The hounds barked but retreated. Dad stood as still as stone, locked in someone's, or something's, embrace.

The laughter died, followed by a booming voice.

"Murder has come, and Murder shall reign, and Murder shall take another again..."

"No!" Mom shrieked, her face instantly wet with tears.

"Blake, what should we do?" Alex yelled.

I have no clue.

But I had to do *something*. "Show yourself, demon!"

The lights in the castle went out, along with the energy in our hands. I opened my palm and tried to reignite it, but it wouldn't work. A loud rumble, followed by a bang, echoed in the vast hallway.

Dad screamed.

Mom shrieked.

Thunder and lightning clapped *inside the castle.*

In the flash of light, I saw a familiar, tall, weird-looking figure approaching from our right, wearing a long, dark cloak.

"Malcolm!" I yelled. "Call off your demon!"

"Malcolm!" Alex screamed. "Stop this, now!" Then, as an afterthought: "I command you, as your queen!"

Malcolm didn't answer. Instead, he flicked one finger and sent a burst of electric blue energy toward Dad.

"No!" I yelled and lunged toward Malcolm at the same time the hounds did, stumbling in the dark. I found his cloak and grabbed it as I went down. Malcolm stood firm, flicked his finger, and sent a burst of energy toward the hounds, throwing them back. They landed in a heap, whining,

"Lucius! Draco! No!" Teddy screamed, scooting around Malcolm toward them.

"Teddy, no!" Alex shouted, but Teddy ignored her and knelt by the hounds piled up in the corner, shaking.

Malcolm flicked his finger and repeatedly pointed a ray of blue energy toward Dad.

Mom and Alex screamed. I twisted around, looking up, expecting to see Dad, his head lobbed off his body, but...

I saw the demon, Murder.

It was far taller than Malcolm and much larger. Its body was deep red, shiny, and covered with fresh blood. It had no head, and its black eyes...were in its chest. The demon let go of my dad and turned the blade toward Malcolm. The hounds righted themselves, snarling and growling at the demon. Teddy, barely visible in the dark, yelled, "Get him, boys!" The hounds lunged just as Malcolm threw a stream of blue light at the demon.

"Dad! Move!" I yelled as he dove for cover, taking Mom and the girls with him.

Thunder and lightning cracked again, the noise so loud I was sure my ears would burst. The demon swiped at the hounds, sending them spiraling backward, nearly bowling Teddy over. It stepped toward Malcolm, its enormous feet leaving a bloody stain on the stone where it had stood. Malcolm flicked a finger again. The electric blue energy burst upward like a lightning bolt and almost torched the ceiling.

I scooted backward, away from what was about to happen, and bumped into Alex.

"Blake, what's going on?"

I shook my head. "I don't know..."

Like spectators in an arena, we watched as Malcolm fought Murder.

Malcolm fired blue lightning energy at the demon, striking it. The demon snarled but fought back, lunging at Malcolm with its blade, missing him, and then striking again, hitting its mark. Malcolm cried out but continued. The hounds circled and attacked and again thrown back. Teddy tended to them, forcing them to stay close by her side before any more damage could be done.

Malcolm flicked several fingers open at once, more and

more energy sparking the room, the thunder in the hall getting louder, the lightning turning toward the demon.

Malcolm's lightening.

He was harnessing energy from the lightning to help kill the demon.

They battled. Malcolm's energy was seemingly no match for the demon's bulk and blade, the blade cutting into Malcolm's clothes and flesh. He grunted, yelled, and cried out several times, each time straightening up and pushing toward the demon, but the demon seemed to overtake him.

Then things turned. Malcolm drove his energy from the tips of his fingers into the demon's eyes, blowing them out from its chest. The demon roared in pain, striking out but unable to see to make his mark.

Malcolm went closer and closer to the demon, concentrating his energy on the demon's middle body while the lightning crashed and burned the demon's arms and legs. The hounds once again stood to attack, this time having the upper hand. The demon dropped its blade and fell back onto the stone floor, so hounds had their way with him before Teddy called them back.

Malcolm stepped closer to the fatally injured demon. With a few more blasts of lightning, the only thing left was black ash.

The stench of burning demon flesh clung to the air.

Malcolm, breathing hard, turned toward us. "Y...your Grace, p...please forgive me."

We all stood shakily. Dad helped Mom off the floor and held her. I helped Alex up. Teddy and the hounds, bloody and battered, joined us. I opened my hand and saw that my powers had returned. I formed an energy ball, lighting up the room. Mom did the same but extinguished them as the castle lights turned on.

Alex stepped closer to Malcolm. "I don't understand, Malcolm. You're a witch? Wasn't it you who summoned the demon in the first place?"

Malcolm shook his large, weird head, holding his side where the demon's blade had hit its mark the hardest. "No, your Grace. I did not."

Alex looked from me back to Malcolm. "Then why did you disappear? When I said I wanted to talk to you about something...you left. Did you think I was going to ask you about the demon?"

"No, your Grace. I...had to leave. I had to prepare."

"Prepare for what? Is that what the altar is for? In the hidden tunnel..." I asked.

Malcolm looked a little startled. "I didn't know you knew about that, your Grace."

Teddy folded her arms across her chest. "I saw you enter the tunnel a few nights ago and followed you. I saw you do your weird ritual stuff and tattled."

"I use the vestibule in the tunnel to commune with and receive guidance from someone who knows you better than anyone, your Grace."

"Who?" Alex asked.

"Me, Alexandra..." A voice came from behind Malcolm. A voice I recognized. As did Alex. The look of confusion on her face surely matched my own.

"Cressy?"

Waldo Cress came out from behind Malcolm, his body and features the gauzy white we were used to seeing. "Yes, Alexandra. Indeed, it is me."

"Cressy, what are you doing here? I...who summoned you?"

"My brother," Cressy said, pointing a thumb toward Malcolm.

"*Your brother?*" A chorus of voices asked in unison.

"Yes. Alexandra, I'd like you to meet my brother, Malcolm Cress."

TWENTY-FIVE

ALEXANDRA

I leaned into Blake, steadying myself. "Cressy. I don't understand. Your brother?"

"Yes, my dear. My brother." Cressy smiled.

"You never mentioned a brother—like—ever."

"I know, my dear. It's just never been...relevant."

Malcolm scoffed and gave Cressy a look. "I mean no disrespect, Malcolm. You are very relevant. You just weren't relevant to the work I had been tasked with bringing Alexandra into her powers."

I frowned at Cressy for calling me a 'task' as though I was a bag of garbage he had to take to the curb, then peppered Malcolm with questions. "Why did you lie about working for Mr. Fellows? And how could you convince me it was Mr. Fellows I was getting references from? Why did you look so strange when you saw Lucas Sheraton in the library? And...why are you even here to begin with?"

Malcolm chuckled and took a step closer. "Allow me to explain, your Grace. First, I recognized Lucas Sheraton as the thought-to-be-dead High Commander of the Order. I was somewhat alarmed."

"Makes sense." I nodded. What about your resume and Mr. Fellows?"

"That's quite simple. You needed protecting."

"From the demon, you mean?"

"No, your Grace. From the hunters. Once you were named Dagon Queen, I knew I needed to step up to protect you from the impending...forgive my choice of words... doom. I created a fake resume and intercepted your call to Mr. Fellows to convince you I was worth the hire. I hope you can forgive me for the deception."

The tension in my neck and shoulders snapped like a guitar string, and I could finally relax...a little. I knew what he meant and thought the choice of the word 'doom' was right on the mark. "After seeing your performance," I pointed to the ash on the floor, "I'm glad for your protection. You're forgiven."

"Thank you, your Grace."

"But," Blake asked, "why all the secrecy? Why not just offer your protection to Alexandra immediately upon her taking to the throne?"

"Being a humble servant was far less obvious to the public—and therefore the Witch Hunters—than being a powerful witch. I was prepared to take on any opponent that threatened our queen, but until that moment of unveiling arose, staying in the background was the best option."

"Nobody but us chickens knows how powerful you are, so your demon-killing secret is safe." Teddy smiled up at Malcolm, who returned it.

"Alexandra," Cressy added, "the demon was a surprise."

Blake slid a comforting hand around my waist. "We're

thrilled you could take care of that, Malcolm. Oddly, our powers were useless, though, and yours weren't. Do either of you know why that would be?"

Malcolm and Cressy looked at each other. "The demon simply had the power to diminish yours. That's why it's been easy to target the other witches. They've been power-less against it." Cressy turned to Alex. "Malcolm isn't a witch, Alexandra. He's a wizard of the highest order. There is truly nothing that can defeat him." Cressy looked at his brother, pride gleaming in his hazy eyes. "Which also made him the perfect bodyguard for Alexandra."

I couldn't help but smile. "Thank you, Malcolm. Are you also...old? Like Cressy was before...?"

"My pleasure, your Grace, and yes. I'm ancient. One of the oldest wizards alive."

"Immortal?"

"No, not immortal. I *can* be killed. But I can also heal quickly from even the deepest wounds." He lifted his shirt to show the recent gash—healing already underway.

"Why was it targeting witches, to begin with, Waldo?" Lucas asked.

Cressy frowned. "We aren't certain. Our only guess is a Witch Hunter was controlling him."

"That's what we thought too!" Teddy said. "But when the hunters drank the wine spiked with truth serum, nobody admitted to it. Poopy buggers."

"Let's remember that the hunters who attended your session were not a full group. Any hunter could have summoned and controlled the demon anywhere." Cressy said. Malcolm agreed.

Blake started pacing. "No, not anywhere in the world. The demon came for my dad shortly after he announced to the Witch Hunters that he was alive and well—and a witch.

That leads me to believe whoever targeted the other witches was the person who sent death threats to my mom and dad all those years ago, and therefore, most likely in Castle Point."

"Excellent deduction, Deputy." Cressy agreed.

"However, as it no longer has a demon to do its dirty work, he or they might end their quest to kill, no?" I asked.

"It's likely the hunter who did the summoning won't let a little thing like killing his demon stop him from destroying more witches. Hopefully, he will slip up and show himself in his desperation."

"But we can't count on that," I argued. "We have a better chance of ending the Witch Hunter reign altogether."

"True, Your Majesty. But the best way to do that would be to return your powers to you," Malcolm said. "Once your powers return, you'll fully control any Witch Hunter in the Order. You can bind them—keep them from ever hunting and harming another witch. The witches would be free to roam the earth, as the Goddess intended."

Cressy came forward, grasping my hands in his translucent ones. "Therefore, I was tasked to be by your side through your lives, my dear child. We knew, without a doubt, that you would one day be able to rectify your mistake as Evelyn of Cumbria. A mistake that you had absolutely no idea you were making, the effort to escape Earl Dagon's grasp and protect yourself. Now you have the chance to change history."

I frowned, bowing my head, my hair hiding the distress I was sure was etched on my face. "That sounds amazing, Cressy, but without Dagon's ancestral blood to complete the spell Magma found, that's decidedly impossible."

"Not true, your Grace." Malcolm shook his head.

I quirked a brow. "What? Why?"

"You've had the required ingredient with you all along."

My heart pulsed. "I have? Oh, my Goddess, what, where?"

Malcolm grasped one hand and turned it over, sliding his thumb along my veins. "Right here."

My entire body shook, my feet threatening to slip out from under me. "My blood?"

"Yes, your Grace. Your blood."

"EEEEEE!" Teddy shrieked, pulling me out of the spell I was suddenly under. "Oh my gosh, Alex, we can make the potion to give you and Penny your powers back!"

I couldn't speak, couldn't think.

This whole time, the ability to regain my powers has been running through my veins.

I looked up at Cressy. "Did you know?"

He shook his head. "No, my dear girl, or I would have told you when Magma found the spell. It was Malcolm who discovered the truth."

I turned to Malcolm. "How? Where?"

"In the tunnels, your Grace. I found the parchment tucked away, deep inside the hidden catacombs of the castle. They kept parts of The Book hidden from the world. The truth."

"Where are the pages?" Blake asked.

"Still in the catacombs. I brought them into the library every night after you had all gone to sleep, using Magma's interpretation of The Book to decode the parchment. The entire story of you, your Grace, is within those pages."

"What do you mean? The story of Evelyn?" I asked,

"No, your Grace. You. Your life—present life—in its entirety."

I peered at him. "I'm afraid I don't get it, Malcolm. Do you mean...a future insight?"

"That's precisely what I mean, your Grace. Perhaps the demon Vine or Earl Dagon must have foretold your future life accounts. Earl Dagon kept that information for himself. He planned to make you queen in this life hundreds of years before you were born."

The room spun. I grasped Blake's arm for support.

This was frigging unreal.

"When the Earl crowned me, he alluded to 'his plan all along.' I thought he meant this lifetime—my lifetime—now. He meant..."

"Since ending your life as Evelyn of Cumbria, yes. I believe he had always regretted burning you on the pyre. His lust for possessing you, body and soul, blinded him. Then it was too late."

A hush fell over the group as everyone took a moment to digest the information. Memories suddenly flooded through me. Not just of this life, but my life as Evelyn, with the Earl, and all at once, I could remember loving him, being afraid of him, running from him, and...dying. Ripples of fear spiked my heart as I relived that life in seconds. Tears flowed, wetting my cheeks and spilling to the floor.

Full circle...

I sobbed. "M...Malcolm, Cressy, th...thank you. For everything." I looked from one man to the other apparition, remembering all the good times I'd had with Cressy, the laughter, the teachings, and the deep sorrow I felt when he crossed over. These odd-looking, amazing, incredible men were my family, my life. And now, so were Teddy, Blake, and his parents.

My heart is full.

Blackjack, who had been hiding Goddess only knows where, jumped into my arms and licked my face with his sandpaper tongue as Blake slid his arm around me, jolting me back to the room. "Teddy, wake Magma and call Penny. We have blood to draw, a potion to make, and a spell to work—"

BOOM.

A loud, crashing bang hit the castle door, startling us all. The hounds snarled and ran to the doors, clawing at them. Blackjack leaped from my arms and shot straight for the nearest hiding spot. I could hear shouting from outside the castle walls.

BOOM.

The large doors shuddered again. The hounds went wild, their protective instincts again kicking into high gear.

"Who—or what—the hell is that?" Lucas asked, walking toward the door.

BOOM.

The doors groaned from the pressure of whatever was hitting it on the other side.

Cressy floated past Lucas and put up a hand, stopping him. "Please, don't open it. Allow me to check." The hounds stepped aside as he vaporized through the door, then quickly returned.

"Cressy, what is it? You're white as a...a ghost." I said.

"Hunters. Hundreds of them, with a battering ram, torches, weapons, and...magic. They're here for you, Alexandra. They're here to kill their queen."

TWENTY-SIX

BLAKE

"They are hitting the door with the battering ram and energy balls. They'll be through soon." although Cressy was an apparition, his breath labored.

My first instinct came from the cop part of my brain. "We should grab whatever weapons we can and go out the back. Flank them from either side of the castle."

"Son, we have our powers. And Malcolm. And the hell hounds. We can face them head-on."

"Right, of course, yes. That." I shook my head, snapping into focus.

You're a witch, you idiot. Use what the Goddess gave you.

BOOM.

The hunters continued to batter and fire at the door, shouting for the queen to surrender.

Malcolm, his large frame towering over Alex, pushed her behind him. "I cannot fight the hunters, sir. My priority is to protect Alexandra—my apologies—I mean the queen,"

"Malcolm, I can protect myself," she insisted.

"Your Grace, may I remind you, you don't yet have your powers back."

"I'll wake Magma! We can make the potion!" Teddy called her hounds, "Lucius, Draco!" The hounds turned from the door, snapping to attention. "Stay here. Protect the castle. Be the ankle biters I know you can be. Injure, but do not kill." The hounds obediently bowed and returned to snarling, snapping, and scratching deep gouges into the door. Teddy bounded toward Magma's room in Teddy's castle wing.

BOOM.

"There isn't enough time! The hunters will be all over the castle, inside and out, in no time." Mom cried.

"I agree. We have to act fast." Dad said.

"I'm afraid he's right, Deputy. They'll be through those doors within minutes." Cressy agreed.

BOOM.

"Blake," Alex grabbed my face, forcing my focus on her. "The people in this castle are far more powerful than those hunters. They're crazy to think they stand a chance against us all...unless..." she looked toward the door, then Cressy. "They have more powers than we realize?"

Cressy floated through the door once again. Several moments later, he reappeared. "Alexandra's right. The hunters... many have recently stolen witch's powers. They aren't just armed, they're dangerous."

"How many of them appear to have powers, Waldo?" Dad asked.

"It looks like over half of them, Lucas."

"There must be hunters from all over the world out there then," I concluded.

"Yes, Son. Many would have flown in for the conclave set for next week."

"Not good," Alex shook her head. "We can't take them all...can we?"

BOOM.

I stood stock still, breathing hard. "I have an idea. Cressy, let us know when they're about to get through the door. When the first wave of hunters falls inside, Malcolm and the hounds can deal with them." Malcolm nodded. "Good. Mom, Dad, and I will force the others back."

"Blake, that's hardly a plan!" Alex yelled. "No. It's too dangerous. There's way more of them than there is of us. I... I have to surrender."

I whipped my head around. "Absolutely not! Why would you even think that was a better plan?"

BOOM.

"Mr. Sheraton is correct, Your Grace. I cannot allow you to surrender." Malcolm said.

Cressy agreed."Alexandra, no. You must go. Hide in the catacombs, anything, go."

"Yes, hide, Alex. Please." I took her face in my hands and kissed her hard. "Please, go. Now."

Alex nodded, tears streaming down her beautiful face, "Injure, don't kill. Promise me?" she looked into all our faces for our agreement. "Blackjack, let's go!" She and her familiar bolted toward the hidden stairway.

Magma and Teddy met her in the hall. Explaining, she slipped into the tunnel while Magma and Teddy scooted into Teddy's lab; I assumed to grab the things they would need to make the potion and return Alex's powers.

Satisfied that Alex was out of the way, I nodded at Cressy to poke his transparent head through the door while

Dad, Malcolm, and I conjured our energy and prepared to battle.

Within moments, Cressy flitted back into the castle, signaling the hunters were about to break through.

BOOM.

The doors creaked, cracked, and split open. Large slivers of wood fell into the castle, narrowly missing us, while the rest of the door stayed on its hinges, burning from the fiery blasts of the witch hunter's stolen powers.

With a great roar, hunters flowed into the castle. The hounds snapped and snarled, biting the ones who were within their reach, pulling them down, and tearing at their cloaks, arms, and legs, injuring but not killing, as their mistress instructed. Screaming, some hunters retreated while others used their new powers to throw clumsy fire-balls at the hounds. Most missed, some hit, but the hounds' scaly skin minimized the damage.

Malcolm threw daggers of blue energy at the hunters, picking them off one by one. The hunters, rendered useless, lay quaking on the floor. Mom, Dad, and I did the same. Our powers had almost the same effect as Malcolm's, but not as intense.

More and more hunters flooded the castle like zombies, stepping over one another to find the flesh of the living inside the domain. Pushing back with our powers, the mob of hunters seemed to retreat, then find their footing and force their way in again. The force and retreat, over and over, was like a wave running onto the sand and back again. Several hunters collapsed when hit with our fire, but a fresh crowd came in just as quickly.

I dodged balls of energy being thrown by hunters with fresh powers. Many of them only got their powers in the last few days or weeks, so some of their energy easily missed me, while others were a close call.

I glanced over at my parents, who, far more seasoned than me, were expertly conjuring and throwing massive balls of energy at hunters and at other energy being thrown their way. Fireworks and bursts of light illuminated the massive hall. The hunters pushed on. The ones recovering from recent energy spikes joined the crowd, many again taken down by a hound or witch, several fleeing the castle, abandoning their brethren.

Growing weary, Mom, Dad, and I slid back further into the castle, but not Malcolm. Despite his recent injuries from fighting the demon, Malcolm seemed to be the only one who had never tired and pushed ahead. Several hunters clever enough to escape the hounds scooted around him, narrowly avoiding the blue lightning coming from his fingers, and ran toward us, plowing deeper into the castle.

"Where's the witch?"

"We want the witch!"

"Give us the witch!" They shouted, scattering around the castle, searching for Alex. I threw as much energy as possible in every direction, trying to hit a hunter before they could run, hitting the odd one, and missing many more. Many hunters yelled insults and shoved me as they pushed past me, making it challenging to conjure my magic quickly.

But many more grew tired of being hit by magic and fled. The number of hunters was diminishing either by being knocked out, fleeing, or threading their way through the castle in search of the queen.

"Sheraton! They've slipped past us!" Malcolm came out of nowhere, sliding beside me, motioning toward the crowd of hunters dispersing—up the staircase, down to the cells, into the rooms—to find Alexandra. The grand hallway was practically bare. The only hunters left were those who lay around, knocked out. Malcolm whispered harshly. "Find the queen. Take her deeper into the catacombs. There is a way out through the furthest tunnel."

"Dad! Mom! Go after the others!"

They nodded their agreement and ran in the direction the other hunters had taken. It would be a dangerous game of hide and seek, but I knew they could hold their own. I took off toward the stairs, tossing energy this way and that, knocking out the hunters who were gaining consciousness.

But I was too late.

Alexandra had slipped out of her hiding spot and stood on the staircase, un-noticed. Her long black hair flowed behind her from the cold winter wind whistling through the castle's front doors. Arms outstretched, she held two red, glowing fireballs in the palms of her hands. Her green eyes pierced the darkness with a determined glow.

"Alex! What are you doing?" I yelled, quickly racing toward her.

"Ending this, Blake!" She yelled back.

"What, how? No! You have to run!"

Hearing me call her name, several hunters raced toward her from all sides, shouting at others to grab her. My parents, who met them with their energy, surprised some. Others were hurrying past or coming from other directions. It was like watching spiders approaching a fly in their web.

What is she thinking? It's...suicide.

I knew her Dagon powers were worthless to use as a hunter, and I knew she knew it too, so I didn't understand...

Realization washed over me. Watching her stand there, poised with Dagon energy, I knew...

TWENTY-SEVEN

ALEXANDRA

B lake kissed me and asked me to hide.

With every fiber of my being, I didn't want to leave him there to fight. I didn't want to lose him. Not now, never.

I love you, Blake.

I couldn't bring myself to say the words out loud, praying to the Goddess that I could tell him, in person, when this was all over.

And it had to be over. Soon.

I reluctantly broke away from his kiss and bolted for the staircase, Blackjack at my heels. Teddy and Magma met as they came down the staircase.

"Alex, where are you going?" Teddy asked.

"The hunters will break into the castle soon, Teddy. I'm going to the catacombs to hide."

"Excellent idea, dear girl. Teddy explained that it's your blood we need for the potion. She and I will work on the potion, then find you when it comes time to add your blood to the mix. We'll have your powers back in no time."

I nodded my thanks, unable to tell them I thought trying would be useless.

The castle was about to be overrun with Witch Hunters.

The Goddess only knew who would survive.

"Please lock yourself in the herbal room and be prepared to fight. Stay safe. If...we lose control of the castle, leave, escape somehow, before the hunters can steal your powers and..." I couldn't finish the sentence, but I didn't have to. Magma and Teddy nodded solemnly and raced to Teddy's herbal room. I found the loose stone and opened the false door under the stairs.

Blackjack and I slid into the tunnel and pushed the door closed just as the castle doors burst open, a thunderous roar of hunters entering. I pressed an ear to the door, listening to the shouts and screams of the men, straining to hear if Blake's voice was one of them.

I couldn't lose him, not now. Not since I found him again.

"Woman, let's gooooo." Blackjack took off down the dimly lit corridor, then stopped and doubled back when he realized I wasn't following. *"What are you doing? You heard the doofus; we need to leave—now!"*

"Blackjack, I can't. I have to figure out a way I can help."

"Help? I hate to state the obvious, but you're useless without your powers."

"Shush!"

I listened intently, and for what seemed like forever, as waves of fear and nausea rode through me.

The shouts and screams approached the stairs.

The hunters had advanced into the castle.

I knew I was supposed to be heading to the catacombs,

but I was riveted to the floor. The door was the only thing between me and my...family, and I couldn't bear to be further away from them.

Did the hunters somehow bypass Blake and the others, or did they...kill them all?

I heard more shouting. It sounded like Blake, but I couldn't be sure.

Not knowing was killing me.

I took a deep breath and pushed the door open just a crack. Hunters scattered about the castle. I could hear them shouting my name, slamming doors, and running across the stone floors. I gingerly pushed the door open further.

Blake pushed and shoved as he fought back, struggling to set his magic ablaze as rapidly as hunters sped by him and disbursed.

As relieved as I was to see him, a swell of panic surged inside me. He needed help, and quickly.

But, I have no powers...except...

I knew what I had to do.

My heart pounding rapidly, I peered up to the staircase and, seeing that it was unoccupied by hunters, quickly left the tunnel and took to the stairs.

I knew that if I threw my Dagon energy directly at a hunter, it would bounce right off them as if they had a protective shield around them—a shield automatically placed by Earl Dagon when the hunters took their oath. Just as the Earl had said—he planned everything. He knew I possessed the Dagon blood and, one day, would try to use that power against the hunters. *His hunters.* He made it impossible for me to do so.

My Dagon ancestral powers may backfire if thrown at Witch Hunters, but they work to hit everything else.

I had a chance to help Blake. I needed to take it.

Standing on the staircase, I stretched my arms wide and conjured enormous, red, fiery energy into my palms. Blake saw me and shouted at me to run, alerting the hunters to my presence.

I stood my ground.

Come and get me, you bastards. I dare you.

As the first hunters approached, I threw my energy toward an object closest to them, a painting, a suit of armor, a statue, pillars—whatever was nearby—and either hit the hunter with it or dropped it into their path, giving me precious seconds to strike at the next one, and the next.

Hunter's cloaks set ablaze with the red Dagon heat. Many dropped and rolled or shed their cloaks, exposing their identity. I threw ball after ball, hitting objects or blasting the ceiling so bits of stone would fall, knocking out a hunter.

It was absolute chaos.

And I loved every minute.

With the guttural cry of every witch who'd ever been tortured and burned on the pyre, I conjured ball after ball of red Dagon heat, blasting my way through the castle, moving down corridors into rooms—a hunter-seeking missile.

I was my very own weapon of mass destruction.

I fully embraced my Dagon powers. Raw, searing energy flowed like lava through me. The last time I embraced it was short and sweet: to save myself and Penny from the pyre.

This time, it was to save us all.

I blasted through the castle, dodging hunters with stolen witch powers and throwing fire or objects in their path. Injured hunters hobbled out of the castle, unwilling to risk their lives for the hunter's stupid cause.

The army of hunters was dwindling rapidly, as was the castle. Large chunks of the ceiling were crumbling and breaking, hitting the upper floors and causing damage to the structure. The walls started caving in, and the castle floors rumbled, weakening with the strain of the falling stone.

It was like the night in the graveyard when Blake begged me to embrace my Dagon powers.

The night I blew up Earl Dagon's headstone.

Now, I was doing the same to the castle.

Earl Dagon's castle.

With ferocity and a blind eye to whoever may be in my way, I pushed on, throwing heat onto every wall, ceiling, and floor...except there weren't any hunters left to stop. Fleeing, they had run from the castle as it crumbled all around us.

"Alex! What are you doing? Stop!" I heard Blake shout, but I couldn't stop.

I didn't want to.

I wanted the castle gone—to destroy the legacy Earl Dagon left behind. The rage burning inside me, spurned on by the Dagon heat in my veins, prevented me from seeing who or what was standing in my way.

I could hear Blake yelling for his parents, Teddy, Magma —even Blackjack—to get out of the castle.

A moment of gratitude for Blake slid through my psyche because I hadn't thought of who was left behind in my all-consuming hate for my ancestry.

My only thought was to destroy.

Soon, the ceiling and back wall of the castle crumbled, a cold winter wind whipping the dust across my face. I ran to the main floor and toward the courtyard, stopping short at the painting of Evelyn.

The painting of *me*.

Summoning the Dagon heat, I threw red fire at the painting, yelling like a banshee as I did so. The energy hit the painting, creating large holes, the flames licking at Evelyn's dress. I looked at her face and saw her deep brown eyes staring back at me. Although the painting depicted Evelyn's face devoid of expression, I could swear the corners of her mouth turned up slightly, and she smiled at me.

A peacefulness fell on my heart.

Goodbye, Evelyn.

The flames consumed her body, reaching higher and higher. Once delicate and serene, Evelyn's face melted and peeled away in ghoulish horror until the gold-gilded frame was the only thing left.

I broke away from the empty frame and continued my destructive rampage. The side walls of the upper floor came crashing down as I blasted my way to the grand entrance and out beyond the castle walls into the chilly night. Turning, I watched the castle quickly crumble; the wind whipping up dust and feeding flames.

The last thing to fall was the tower. It crumpled in on itself with a great groan, taking what remained of Evelyn of Cumbria's belongings.

A massive plume of dust kicked up from the heap, blinding me from the view of the remains. I raised a hand to shield my eyes from the specks of debris. As the dust and flames settled, a figure slowly emerged. It was hazy at first, then more apparent. I thought perhaps it was a hunter who had been left behind, but...no.

It was Earl Dagon.

CHAPTER

TWENTY-EIGHT

BLAKE

I love you too, Alex.

I had heard her thoughts as she raced to the hidden tunnel, but had no time to reach out to grab her, hold her, and kiss her one more time.

I was fighting for our lives.

I was fighting against the hunters who had been my friends. The guys I grew up with, worked with, went to footfall games, and hung out with.

Their visceral rage against Alexandra astounded me. They had become beasts on a mission to destroy the one good thing I had found in this world. Their behavior was...

Categorically evil.

But I fought because what else could I do? I had to protect Alex.

And my true legacy—as a witch.

I was almost surprised when I saw that the hunter's only mission was to find and kill Alex. Although they fought with me, no one tried to capture me or my parents and steal our powers for themselves.

They were rabid dogs after the sole morsel of purity within the castle walls.

But Alex destroyed those walls.

I watched intently as she used her fiery powers to strike at the castle, harming or stopping the hunters for a short time until her rampage sent them running or limping from further danger. She didn't stop until there was nothing left. Many of the hunters—mainly those without powers of their own—fled the castle and didn't stop running until they were well out of the line of fire.

Now, we all stood, speechless, as the dust settled...

And Earl Dagon appeared.

CHAPTER
TWENTY-NINE

ALEXANDRA

"*EVELYN, WHAT HAVE YOU DONE?*" Dagon's filmy lips moved, but the wind carried his booming voice from all directions.

I instinctively ducked, attempting to avoid the voice, then leaped onto a heap of rubble that used to be the entrance to the castle and yelled at the ghost of my long-dead oppressor. *"I'm not your Evelyn! I never was. Your reign has ended, Dagon, as has mine. The last remaining piece of you is this castle, and it's gone. So should you be!"*

The Earl's ghost stared at me, his brow creasing, then turned in a slow circle, surveying the crumbled pieces of his legacy. I saw his eerie face turn a bright red as he turned back to me. He raised his arms, balling his large hands into fists, and *roared.*

His apparition grew, swelling with anger. His dark, brooding eyes turned completely black. He launched from his position, hovering over the rubble that was once the courtyard, and flew toward me.

Anxious fear rippled over my heart, but I stood firm, balling my fists at my side, awaiting his grim presence. Dagon's spectral spirit stopped short of me; his fists balled so tightly that his ghostly knuckles turned white. Through gritted teeth, he spat, *"You disappoint me, Alexandra. I gave you the castle and the crown, and, once again, you refuse me, destroying my legacy in the process."*

I jutted my chin toward him. "I don't give two shits whether I disappointed you, you asshole. I'm not yours. I never should have been and never will be again. If I have to make a deal with the devil himself to ensure that we will never cross paths again in this life or any other, I'll do it."

The intensity of his anger was etched in his gauzy features.

I held my ground. We stared at each other in a twisted contest.

"You defy me, yet I feel compelled to remind you that you once loved me, Evelyn." Dagon forcefully pushed vivid images into my mind, reminding me of the past when Evelyn, a young witch, was drawn to the Earl's gentlemanly and kind nature. The wealthy Earl clearly loved the naïve woman I once was, and we enjoyed many memorable moments together.

"You see? We once had a love that knew no boundaries of time, Evelyn. And yet, you ran. You forced me to go after you, to capture you, and later destroy you. You did that, Evelyn, and you are doing it again. We were meant to be together. Forever."

Rage rumbled inside me. My fingernails pierced the flesh of my palm. I could feel the warmth of my blood dripping through the fingers of my clenched fist. "That's total bullshit, you incredible asshole. I may have loved you as a naive girl, but that quickly changed when you showed me your true nature." I pushed my memories of that life toward the Earl. The abuse, both physical and verbal, and the terror, mixed with the hatred I knew after some years within his grasp. And, finally, the freedom I felt when I ran, escaping him, and the pain I went through when he captured me and burned me alive on the pyre.

The Earl's eerie features, a translucent stone, processing the memories I shared with him. His black eyes retreated to their usual dark shade, flicking over my face. His brow furrowed, but his hands unclenched and relaxed at his sides. Finally, his features softened, but mine held firm as I continued to push memory after memory of his torture and abuse toward him, battling the barrier of his true, obsessive, evil nature with that of my own gentle, loving one.

"Evelyn, my intentions toward you were never to hurt you. You were the reason I behaved so badly toward you. You and your ideals." Firelight flittered in Dagon's dead eyes.

I stood my ground, piercing his gaze with my own. "My desire for freedom, you mean? My desire to *not* live with an oppressive, abusive, egotistical maniac?"

Dagon growled. *"I loved you, Evelyn. More than anyone has loved another. Ever."*

"You had a shitty way of showing it." I pushed the feelings that came with every bruise, every fear, every terror I felt during my time with him through my living, beating heart and into his dead one. Warm tears streamed down my face, turning to ice in an instant as I relived the pain of our being together. I held his gauzy stare, watching for any sliver of remorse. I pushed harder, the memories slicing through me like the sharpest blade, attempting to pierce the heart of pure evil.

At last, I crumbled and fell to my knees, panting.

"Evelyn, I..."

I looked up at him, gritting my teeth. *"My name is Alexandra."*

The hard edge of Dagon's expression changed; his features softened and shifted to a younger Earl Dagon—the one I recalled as gentle, even loving. The same Dagon I had been attracted to at the beginning of our life together when we fell madly, deeply in love.

I wanted to reach out, touch his gauzy frame, and hold his massive hand in mine, but I held back, instead rising to my feet again. He held my gaze for a moment before his shoulders slumped, his head bowed, and he spoke softly. *"Very well, Alexandra. You win. You may have your freedom. From me, from your powers, from your ancestry. You are free."* He turned abruptly and slowly floated away, turning once to wave goodbye.

I gawked at the apparition as it slowly faded, shock registering in my appendages, the previous heat of anger cooling with the night air. I tried to take a breath, but my lungs had forgotten how.

Did he say what I think he said?

I'm...free?

Could it be that easy?

But it wasn't. It hadn't been. In the span of a few minutes, I had relived every hurt he had caused, every torture he had doled out, all to make him *see*.

Could I trust that he had truly gotten the message?

And what happens now?

I shivered. The involuntary shivers turned to trembles, and my body wracked as waves of the familiar Dagon heat spread through me but were not summoned *by* me. The heat flowed through my veins and landed with a painful, itchy sensation in my hands. I stared at them, red-hot as coals in my maniacal castle destruction, now marked with ragged fingernail cuts and blood. Balls of red energy formed in my palms, not of my own doing. My arms were yanked up high by an invisible source as the oppressive Dagon energy was pulled from my being.

Wave after wave of red-hot heat shot up from my fingers and into the sky. My body rocked and shuddered with each rolling wave—an ongoing shock of electric, painful energy.

I opened my mouth, screamed, and dropped to my knees.

Higher and higher, the energy leaped from my body and rode the crisp winter wind into the cosmos and beyond. I was, once again, losing my powers. Only this time, the Dagon powers were being pulled from my being. I wanted to laugh, cry, and scream as the pulsing energy swept from my body. Barely breathing, I was consumed by the dark force being ripped from me for what seemed like hours.

And then, as suddenly as it had begun, it was gone.

My body rapidly cooled from my toes up my legs, into my body, and down my arms into my hand, the Dagon heat dissipating quietly—the chill calming the painful extraction of my once hated powers.

Exponential relief flooded through me. I smiled, looking into the clear night sky—then laughed maniacally.

I couldn't stop laughing. I laughed so hard I had to hold my sides. I lifted my head to the sky and laughed, tears streaming down my face.

For the first time...ever...I felt...*alive*.

THIRTY

BLAKE

Many hunters stayed behind to watch Earl Dagon strip Alex's powers. They stood there, dumbfounded and silent. Too tired to fight and seemingly too tired to care.

When Earl Dagon appeared, argued, and then released her ancestral burden, I could only imagine her feelings—first, the pain, then...nothing. Mom and Dad held me back when I tried to run to her, pull her from the torment Earl Dagon was putting her through.

"You cannot stop it, Son. Let him take her powers. Stopping it would cause greater harm to Alex." He explained.

So I watched her writhe in pain, her energy being yanked from her body. I hadn't been there the night Earl Dagon stripped her of her witchy powers, but I could only imagine the process was the same. I prayed to the Goddess that she would be okay.

"Alex!" I shouted. She turned toward me but remained perched on the rubble.

"Blake! Did you see it? Dagon stripped my powers!"

"Yes, I saw. Get down from there, please. Before you fall."

She carefully stepped off the rubble she was perched on and quickly approached me.

"Did you get everyone out in time?" she asked.

"Yes. Barely. What were you thinking?" I glanced at the dusty piles of stone where a castle once stood.

"I...wasn't. "I'm...sorry. I couldn't...help myself. Those powers...consumed me...but now they're gone." The winter chill froze the tears on her cheeks into icicles as she reached for her vial earring to pull at—the adorable nervous habit I'd come to love. "My earring of Cressy's ashes! It's...gone." She flicked her head around, hoping to see it in the rubble. "It must have slipped off when I...oh!" Tears welled in her eyes.

"Alex, it's okay. You hardly need it. You can talk to Cressy anytime you want. C'mere." Taking her hand, I welcomed her warmth as we embraced. I glanced down at her beautiful face, ruddy with a mix of the chill of the air and splashes of blood and dirt. Blackjack came out of hiding and rubbed against her leg. Alex scooped him up and held him close.

I pulled them both toward me. Holding Alex in the chilly winter air, I could finally relax.

"Geez, witch bitch. Remind me never to piss you off." Penny approached us, stepping over a mix of stone and castle artifacts strewn everywhere.

"Penny!" Alex hugged her tight, squishing a meowing cat in the middle. "Did you see...everything?"

"I saw enough. Teddy called me earlier and told me—no, commanded me—to get my delicious booty over here. But..." she looked around, scratching her head, "there's no more 'here' to get to..."

We laughed.

"So, Dagon took your powers, eh? What an enormous dick-wad. He just won't let you have *any* fun."

"Yup. My powers are gone. All of them." I glanced around the rubble. "Guess I'll have to rebuild if I plan on turning this into a museum in remembrance of the Witch Trials..." I groaned.

I wanted to laugh or cry for her. I couldn't decide which to do first.

"It's okay," I said, kissing her head. "We can rebuild it into something beautiful. Something the families of the tortured witches can be proud to visit. Right now, Teddy and Magma have something for you..."

"What is it? Did they...?"

"Finished the potion, yes. It only needs one last ingredient..."

Alex smiled up at me.

"What potion? What ingredient? What are you and the big hulky, sweaty boy talking about?" Penny asked.

"Magma found an interpretation in The Book to get our powers back, Pen."

"Well, it's about time. Does it *have* to be another potion? The last one was super gross, dude."

"Hey!" Teddy scolded from behind us. "Not fair. I tried real hard on that one."

"Sorry, Ted, no offense," Penny called over her shoulder before making a stinky gagging face at us. "What's the ingredient?" she dropped her voice to a whisper, "I hope whatever it is, it tastes better this time..."

"It's my blood," Alex interrupted.

Penny made a face and gagged again. "Uh...hard pass."

We laughed so hard our cheeks hurt, and tears streamed down our faces.

Relieved laughter and tears.

Alex may have lost her powers, but she won her war.

"Lucas!" Gordon Roberts called out to my dad, who turned toward him, smiling. Gordon wasn't present for the Witch Hunters...hunt. At least, not that I saw.

"Gordon!"

"Looks like I missed quite a show."

"You did, my old friend. The rebel Witch Hunters were after Alexandra."

"But our queen is safe, I see."

Alex and I walked toward Dad and Gordon, stepping over loose debris.

"Not a queen, Gordon. And no longer a Dagon ancestor. I'm just...Alex." She smiled. "I may not be Queen of the Witch Hunters—or even a witch—but I am definitely laying charges against all the hunters involved in tonight's...escapade. And I want those who have stolen a witch's powers brought to justice. I changed the law after becoming queen, Gordon. The law is the law."

I peered around at the hunters who had lingered after the others had run. It wouldn't be easy to control a group of men who felt justified in their actions after hundreds of years of tradition—let alone find all of those who took part in the plot to kill their queen. Alex had shifted everyone's reality when Earl Dagon crowned her and rewrote history.

Gordon nodded solemnly. "Understood. Of course. We have our work cut out for us, Deputy Sheriff Sheraton." He said, addressing me.

Mom, Teddy, Penny, and Magma came closer, group hugs all around. Malcolm stood stoically beside our little crew until Penny reached out and, grabbing his arm, forcibly pulled him into the hug.

It's over.

Or so I thought.

Dad broke away from our little clan and, smiling, stepped closer to Gordon, hand outstretched—a sign of forgiveness and solidarity between old friends.

His smile faded as Gordon pulled a large blade from under his coat.

The same blade the demon, Murder, had held against Dad's neck.

Gordon lunged, driving the blade toward Dad's heart.

"No!" I screamed. I leaped toward Dad, putting myself in the direct line of Gordon's thrust. The blade's tip pierced me in the chest. Pain seared through me, my hand instinctively clasping my chest, and I was thrown back, hitting Dad and landing in a heap on top of him.

The moments before and after Gordon stabbed me seemed to run in agonizingly slow motion.

Warm blood oozed onto my shirt and then quickly cooled in the night air. Alexandra was instantly by my side, holding her hand over the wound, shouting my name. Penny kneeled beside her, doing the same and yelling at someone to call 911.

Mom shrieked and threw a ball of energy toward Gordon, who quickly ducked, avoiding the blaze.

Gordon stepped closer. "It's no use, Meredith. You're surrounded."

Holding my chest, I struggled to get off of Dad while glancing around.

The Witch Hunters who stayed behind had circled our little party while our guard was down.

"Gordon! What are you *doing*?" Dad asked, helping me

sit up. Alex sat behind me, supporting my back. Malcolm and the other witches surrounded us protectively—a circle within a circle.

"Taking care of the thing I failed at twenty years ago." Gordon sneered.

"It was you," I stated, pointing to the blade in his hands. "You were the one who summoned the demon and tried to kill my parents. You killed those other witches."

Gordon nodded slowly.

"But, why, Gordon?" Dad asked. "We were...friends."

Gordon spat, "Friends? You were a witch infiltrating the Order! You and your witch friends! When I found out, the only choice I had was to end you. All of you. I summoned the demon Murder for help, and it was working! You weren't my friend, Lucas. You were my enemy. You always have been and always will be. And now, you must die."

Our little group raised their energy, ready to attack.

Gordon signaled the Witch Hunters to do the same.

I could barely move, my breath coming in shallow spurts. The shooting pain in my chest left me with hardly enough energy to fight back. Fear slipped through me when I realized how outnumbered we were. To survive would take a miracle straight from the Goddess herself. I cringed and watched each hunter spread their arms, palms up, to ignite their energy in unison.

But none of them could.

Confused glances at their hands and each other, the hunters tried repeatedly, flicking their fingers, opening and closing their palms.

Nothing.

"What is the matter with you!" Gordon shrieked at the hunters.

"It's not working, Commander!" One hunter yelled. "Our powers have..."

"Been stripped." Alex breathed. She opened her palm, perhaps willing her powers to return, but no. She looked at me. "Dagon must have stripped their powers when he stripped mine..."

A calm relief flooded through me; only the pain point of the stab wound was evident.

My ears rang, and the world around me faded to black...

THIRTY-ONE

ALEXANDRA

M y heart clenched when I saw the blade pierce Blake's chest.

No!

I fell beside him, pressing a hand to the entry point, unable to tell if the wound was superficial or deep. Blood spread rapidly across his shirt, the coppery scent lodging deeply into my mind for my subconscious to recall repeatedly in the future. My hands were red from holding Blake's chest and blue from the cold, but I didn't care.

Everything happened around me in a vacuum. Voices and faces were dull, speaking in monotone English, but it may as well have been a foreign language. Penny grabbed my shoulders, shaking me, yelling words I couldn't hear. I could sense the frosty night air whipping up all around us, but I was already numb from the shock and confusion of what was happening.

When Gordon admitted to being the one who

summoned the demon, Murder, I wished beyond reason for my Dagon powers back so I could blast the son-of-a-bitch straight to hell.

But, when the Witch Hunters couldn't summon the powers they had recently stolen, a calmness and a sweet sense of justification swept over me. The foreboding feeling of impending doom vanished. Although I did not know if the hunters could steal a fresh set of powers from a witch in the future, I remained optimistic that their reign of terror had ended.

Malcolm, Lucas, Meredith, and Magma quickly bound Gordon and the remaining hunters with their magic, making them immovable, until they could connect with the trusted authorities who could take them away to face their punishment later.

For the moment, my focus was on Blake.

While the others dealt with the hunters, Teddy called 911, and Penny tended to Blake's wounds until the ambulance arrived. I rode to the hospital with Penny and Blake—still passed out and losing blood. They wheeled him into emergency and then quickly into surgery. Penny took care of admittance, coming to the waiting room to be with me afterward. She tried to convince me everything would be okay, that Blake had the best surgeon in the world, that he was in expert hands.

I wanted to believe her, but I couldn't. Not until I saw him for myself.

I paced the waiting room floor, wearing the already threadbare carpet to the point of no return. Lucas, Meredith, Magma, and Malcolm joined us in the waiting room after they had ensured Gordon and the others were under lock and key.

"Have you seen the doctor, Alexandra? Is my boy okay?" Meredith asked, rushing into the waiting room.

My throat had gone dry. "Nothing yet." I rasped, "He's still in surgery. Are the others locked up?"

Lucas nodded. The lines on his face deeper with the stress of the past days. "The cells at the department are bursting, but they're in there."

"Can we trust that the current deputies won't release them? So many of them are hunters themselves..."

"I've contacted the witches that I know are in sheriff positions in Dagon County. It took me a minute to explain how we were back from the dead, but once I did, they agreed to assign deputy witches on the case and move the prisoners to other locations—until they set a trial date."

I nodded. "Thank you, Lucas. We're in for some massive changes in this world."

"Indeed we are," he agreed.

We all sat, exhausted, waiting for news of Blake's condition.

At some point—I didn't know when—Penny's wife, Cathy, had joined our little party. She hugged me and said some words I couldn't respond to without bursting into tears before sitting beside Penny, holding her hand and listening as Penny explained everything.

I looked into the face of each person sitting, waiting for the same news. These people were my family now. A deep sense of gratitude warmed the coldest part of my heart. The part that was steely from wanting too much—from ever hoping I could have a normal life—a life without worrying that I would end up on the pyre because of my craft. A life no longer of solitude to ensure the Dagon blood ended with me, but having the life I had longed for.

One that, perhaps, *didn't* include being a witch.

One that included having a child.

If Blake survived, that is.

And he wanted to be with me, which, I was pretty sure, he did.

I closed my eyes and willed my thoughts and energy to him straight from my heart center to his.

Please be okay, Blake. Please be okay.

The thought of a world without Blake left a void in my soul. My mind reeled with a kaleidoscope of images, from attending Blake's funeral to being alive to having children with him, becoming Sheriff, and embracing his powers for good.

Because he *had powers.*

What would life with Blake be like if I *weren't* a witch?

What if I didn't drink the potion to regain my powers?

I imagined my everyday life—the life I'd missed since moving into the castle. The thought of opening my therapy practice and crafting personal care products for my apothecary again sent an excited thrill through me. Would I miss using my powers to perform simple, mundane tasks? If I couldn't, I'd have to ask Teddy—or Blake—to add the dash of magic to the products like I always had when I created them, so that wouldn't be too bad.

What about using my powers to expel negative energy and entities from my clients? Assuming I would re-open my practice once...things...settled down.

That thought gave me pause.

Although my magic always had to be hidden, and my clients didn't know I used it to extract the beings possessing them, I didn't know any other way to do that without using magic.

Without magic, I'd be a regular therapist.

I'd be a regular...person.

And Blake would be a witch, battling evil and doing good in the world.

Because even though the Witch Hunters had lost their stolen powers, it didn't mean we wouldn't have a world-wide revolt to deal with. We were on the cusp of a new world. Anything could happen.

Could I stand by and watch from the sidelines as Blake —and my new family—battled?

I glanced at each of them once more, stopping at Meredith. She lifted her head off Lucas's shoulder and gave me a little smile, which I returned. She was an amazing mother, despite having fled for twenty years; but because of it—a mother who sacrificed having a life with her child to protect him.

A deep longing for a mother like Meredith tugged at me.

But I had a mother.

One that needed to get out from under a demon's hex.

And to do so required magic.

A lot of magic.

Suddenly, the decision of whether to drink the potion was made.

It was so simple. I longed for a family. One that included my mother. One that included magic.

I leaned back in the uncomfortable waiting room chair and closed my eyes. The pieces of my life slipped into place. I had a plan. I had a purpose.

Now, I only needed Blake to be okay.

Finally, the surgeon approached. I jumped up, my jaw set, trying to read his eyes. His expression gave nothing away other than sheer exhaustion from hours of surgery.

"Doctor? Is my son okay?" Meredith asked, standing beside me. Lucas wrapped his arm around her for support.

Finally, his expression shifted, and he smiled. My heart leaped. "He's going to be fine. But it was a close call. The knife was only a fraction of an inch away from piercing his heart."

I was instantly soaked in relief, sat down, and sobbed.

THIRTY-TWO

BLAKE

unters surrounded me, holding me back as they killed everyone in my family. I could see Alexandra's beautiful face twisted into a painful scream as she was run through with Murder's blade. Her body fell to a lifeless heap at my feet. I opened my mouth to scream, but no sound escaped. My heart beat faster, then seemed to beat right out of my chest. I looked down, seeing my heart, not understanding how it could be on the outside of me, exposed for the hunters to find easily. They circled me, pointing, laughing, and jeering at my exposed heart. Gordon pointed the blade toward me and came closer and closer until the tip of the blade touched my heart. An evil grin spread over his face as he pushed.

I heard voices.

Was it the hunters?

I strained to hear further.

My name.

Someone was calling my name.

"Blake? Can you hear me? Wake up."

Who was that? Alex? But...she was dead, no?

The scent of roses mixed with...mud? Dirt? Smoke? Hit my senses.

Alexandra.

"Blake, sweetheart, open your eyes."

Mom?

I could feel someone holding my hand—no, hands. And someone else ran a hand over my head. And then I felt hands resting on my feet, arms, and legs. It was an octopus of hands laid all over me. I could feel the warm sensation of healing energy running through me, giving me strength.

I opened my eyes.

The sharp light of day pierced my vision. Blinking, it took several seconds for my vision to clear.

Everyone I loved surrounded me. Their smiling, dirty, sooty, blood-spattered faces were the most beautiful faces I'd ever seen.

Especially Alex's.

She smiled, then leaned forward, kissing my lips softly. I tried returning the kiss but couldn't work my lips.

Mom kissed my forehead first, then Dad did.

I moved my tongue around my mouth, conjuring saliva. Opening my mouth, I rasped, "What happened?"

Dad answered. "Gordon stabbed you with Murder's blade, Son. It nearly hit your heart. You were in surgery for quite a while, but you'll be fine."

I smiled. Or I tried to. My head was dizzy. My body responded to sensations. Prickly heat rode through my veins and into my heart.

My heart? The two-faced bastard almost hit my heart.

On cue, a pain in my chest ripped through me, and I

winced. Penny shimmied beside Alex. "You feeling some pain in your chest, Blake?"

I nodded slowly.

"Okee dokee, tough guy. I'll give you a little happy juice, and you'll be floating on a cloud in no time." She turned some dial on the tube that flowed from a plastic bag into my veins.

Penny was being so nice. Not the Penny I knew. I liked this Penny.

A warm, relaxed sensation fell over me.

Mom kissed my forehead again, saying they'd let me rest and return later.

Everyone left the room except for Alex.

She leaned over again, placing small kisses all over my face.

It was pretty sweet.

"You're my hero, Blake."

I looked into her beautiful green eyes and wanted to giggle, but I felt too sleepy. I whispered.

"No, Alexandra. I'm *your* hero."

"That's what I just said."

"Oh." Maybe I had that wrong. Who was who's hero?

"Blake?"

"Yeah?"

"Good thing you're cute."

THIRTY-THREE

ALEXANDRA

Blake was in the hospital for about a week. Between daily visits, I reopened my house, removing the dust covers, cleaning, and making Lucas and Meredith as comfortable as possible. Blake's apartment was only one bedroom, too cramped for his parents to stay there, so I insisted they stay with me.

Magma refused to leave until she partook in the ceremony to return my powers. I told everyone I didn't want to do that until Blake was present, which they all accepted. Truthfully, I was still tackling the idea of not having my powers returned at all, which I honestly thought I could live without—except where my mother and her demon hex were concerned.

Malcolm insisted on still protecting me—even though Lucas and Meredith were close by—but his home was in another county, so he took the downstairs bedroom.

Teddy and her hounds—glamored, of course—stayed with Penny and Cathy until she could find a suitable place to live. Unfortunately, Teddy's belongings were buried in the rubble that used to be Castle Dagon. I had only brought the bare necessities, so I had plenty of clothes in the closet at home.

I gathered everything I knew would fit Teddy, brought them to her, paid her a generous bonus, and gave her a raise to find a house with a large yard for the hounds and furnish it.

I spent as much time with Blake as possible that week, not wanting to reopen my practice until I knew Blake was okay and the 'new world' was a bit more stable. Malcolm insisted on following me everywhere, even to the hospital. He would stand sentry outside Blake's hospital room door while I visited.

I often made Blake homemade broth and spooned it to him.

"You're quite the package," he told me between spoonfuls. "Good looking, superb cook, passionate, amazing kisser…"

I frigging blush. "Thanks." I smile, wiping his chin.

"You don't have to feed me, though; I'm well enough to spoon my soup."

I blush again. "Oh, of course…I just…"

"Want to take care of me? I get it. It's mutual." He winks. "I'm being released today."

That surprised me. "Really? You're well enough?"

"Doc Holloway seems to think so."

"Well…that's good then."

"You don't seem too pleased. Sad you won't be able to bring me soup anymore? I could come over for regular spoon feedings if you'd like." He grins. "And, maybe other things…?"

I blush again, the heat from my groin hitting my face, turning me at least fifty shades of red, I was sure.

For Goddess's sake, get yourself together.

"Ha. That's okay. I'm sure you can feed yourself. As for the other 'things,' your parents live with me now, so..."

He nodded and wiggled his eyebrows. "So, I better get to work finding them a place to live."

I blushed again. Putting the soup aside, I excused myself and went to the bathroom to splash cold water on my face. When I returned, Blake was sitting on the side of the bed, pulling on the underwear, pants, and shirt his mother had brought from his apartment. I glanced away. He laughed.

"I'm not shy. Also, I'm already decent, so you don't have to be shy either."

I looked at him, smiling, and grabbed my things. "I guess you're ready? I'll get the discharge nurse."

Malcolm pulled my car around to the hospital entrance while they discharged Blake, and I wheeled him out to the snowy curb. Helping him into the back seat, I reached for his seatbelt and snapped it in. He grabbed hold of either side of my face and planted a gentle kiss on my lips.

It took all of my energy not to jump into his lap. I closed the door and got on the other side, beside him. Malcolm drove.

"Your place or mine?" I asked, willing the heat to stay in my groin, not rush to my cheeks.

"Yours. I'd like to see everyone. Plus, we must plan the ceremony to regain your powers."

I nodded but said nothing.

"Magma still has the potion?"

"Yes, it's in my apothecary at home."

"Just needs one last ingredient..."

"Yeah..."

Blake placed a hand on mine. Prickly heat rose up my arm. "You don't sound too happy about getting your powers back. Everything okay?"

I glanced at him, gave a small smile, and nodded. "Yeah, okay, I guess. I..."

Blake finished my sentence. "Haven't decided if you want them back or not."

I nodded again. Tears stung my eyes. I wiped at them. "You reading my mind?"

"Apparently, it comes with the Sheraton territory. Sorry."

"It's fine. Could come in handy, I suppose."

"I thought you were excited to have your powers back? It frustrated you about losing them for so long..."

"True. I guess I was wondering what a normal life would be like. That maybe I'd prefer that over being a witch again."

Blake pulled my hand to his lap, holding it in both hands. "Can I ask you something? I promise not to read your mind for the answer."

My eyebrows shot up. "Sure, I guess?"

"Do you want to be with me, Alex?"

The question momentarily stunned me. I had been dreaming of a life with Blake in my solitary thoughts. I hadn't considered that he would question me about it. I answered quietly, with my own question, "Do you want to be with me?"

Blake smiled and nodded. "More than you know."

I nodded and smiled back, my heart beating a little faster. "I feel the same way."

"Then you must consider that life with me will never be

'normal.' I'm a witch, Alex. I only embraced my powers weeks ago and don't intend to give that up. For anyone."

I looked past Blake out the car window, the snow falling softly, coating the world with a fresh perspective. A cleansing that it desperately needed.

I thought about life with my powers, how natural it felt to be a witch, and life without them, how empty and broken I had felt when Dagon stripped them from me.

I thought about the world now, how the hunters would have to adapt to a world where witches walked freely, without fear, and realized that I wanted that freedom. I wanted to stand with my brother and sister witches and experience the world differently.

The thought was the ice pick to my frozen heart. I smiled widely at Blake. Leaning over to kiss him, I pushed my thoughts to his mind.

Time to finish that potion...

THIRTY-FOUR

BLAKE

Everyone but me shuffled the living room furniture and created an altar. Candles lit up the room. I was still sore from surgery and under the doctor's order not to exert myself, so I sat on the chaise, watching.

The only person not in attendance was Penny.

As Alex had figured, Penny was enjoying her life with Cathy, free of magic. When she came over to discuss it, she said, "I'm a hugger now, Alex. I *hug* people! Can you believe it? I could never do that before when my psychic abilities were intact. I'd feel their pain and see their future whenever I touched someone. I don't want to know whether one of my patients will die tomorrow, Alex. I want to grow old with Cathy and not know when we will cross over. I want a normal life. Whatever that looks like."

"I understand, of course. You'll always be my best friend. Powers would never change that." Alex hugged her.

Penny pushed her away, grasped her by the shoulders, one eyebrow cocked. "What a dumb thing to say. Of *course,* we'll always be besties. You're not planning to move to the moon anytime soon, are ya?" I laughed and shook my head. "Then it's settled. You and the hottie Sheriff can have a batch of witchy babies, and Cathy and I will be happy, normal aunties. Deal?"

Alex glanced at me, her cheeks flushed.

I winked, laughing. "Deal. Although calling yourself normal, even without your powers, is a bit of a stretch."

"Touche, witch bitch number two. Touche."

Blackjack circled the room, meowing. Scooping him up and stroking his head, Alex asked if he was okay with her getting her powers back. I could hear his thoughts.

"Woman. It's who you are. You're a High Priestess, remember? The witching world will expect their leader to navigate and guide them in the new world. Also, there's the matter of your mother. The more witches to remove her curse, the merrier."

Alex hugged him close. He rubbed his head against her chin and purred. "Thanks, Blackjack."

"I could even get on board with having the doofus Sheriff around more if it meant you would have a witchy companion. Just warn me if you plan to push out a pack of wailing babies. That might be my cue to join the Man on the other side."

"Hey! Not nice to call people names, Mr. Farty Cat." I scolded, laughing.

"Not nice to listen in on other people's conversations, Doofus!" Blackjack snarked back.

Alex frowned at his mention of leaving her to be with Cressy but seeing as Blackjack had already been with her for thirty years, she supposed she could let him go and keep Cressy company in the ethers.

"Cressy! I nearly forgot to ask you all to summon my mentor for the ceremony." Alex looked around the room.

"I'm already here."

Hearing the voice, she jumped and turned, dropping Blackjack, who gave a little screech and ran to Alex's mentor.

"Cressy? You're here! We hadn't even summoned you."

Malcolm and Cressy chuckled. Malcolm's voice was lower and more robust than Cressy's etheric one, so he sounded a bit like a Harley Davidson was in the room.

She glanced from one to the other. "What's so funny?"

Malcolm answered. "You only need to call his name, Alexandra. He will be here."

She quirked an adorable eyebrow. "Since when?"

Cressy smiled, clasping his hands behind his back. "Since always. I knew how much you enjoyed the summoning ritual, so I didn't have the heart to tell you it wasn't necessary."

Alex folded her arms and huffed. "You could have saved me the trouble!"

"Now, now, my dear. Where would be the fun in that?"

Everyone laughed.

THIRTY-FIVE

ALEXANDRA

I had no expectations of what it would feel like to regain my powers.

I had only hoped it wasn't as painful as losing them.

It wasn't.

As everyone—*my family*—including Cressy and Blackjack, formed a circle around me, I glanced around, meeting everyone's eyes. Instantly, my heart warmed to peace, gratitude, and love.

Magma raised her hands in the air and chanted,

"Goddess good, Goddess great, we gather here to appreciate,
The witch she was and soon will be,
We ask you to grant great powers to thee."

A swirling vortex of white-gold energy formed above my head. I looked up, watching as the vortex widened and tiny sparks of golden light sprinkled down on me. Like delicate kisses, the energy touched my skin, my face, and my head, the sparks growing in size and abundance as the group chanted:

"Goddess good, Goddess great, by cauldron, potion and athame,
Return this witch's powers from whence they came."

Magma stepped closer to me as the other continued the chant, rhythmically swaying. She grasped one of my hands, took my blade—the athame Cressy had given me as a child —and pushed it against my palm. I breathed as the athame's sharp stab pierced my palm. Blood pooled instantly.

Holding my palm upright, Magma clasped the vial of potion she and Teddy had created at the castle. Keeping it under my palm, she clasped my hand into a fist and tipped it, spilling three drops of blood into the vial. I pulled my hand back as she moved the vial in a circular motion, mixing the blood into the potion.

The sparks of energy above my head spun into the vial, creating a cyclone. The potion glowed yellow, orange, and red. Magma held the potion up to my face and pressed it against my lips. I took a deep breath, grasped the vial, tipped it back, and, with one great swallow, allowed the potion to run down my throat.

Looking down at my arms, I saw swirling, warm energy running through my veins, turning them yellow, orange, and gold as the potion flowed through me. The brew pushed further into my being with every pump of my heart until the glow in my veins and the rhythm of my heart finally settled to a regular pace.

The room fell silent. I glanced around at the witches, each with a broad smile on their faces.

"Is that it? It's done?"

Soft chuckles fell all around.

"That's it, dear one," Magma answered. "Your powers have been returned.

I raised an eyebrow and turned toward Cressy. "Really, Cress? That's it? I have my powers back?"

Cressy laughed. "Yes, my dear. What, pray tell, were you expecting?"

"I don't know...more...pain, perhaps? More...fireworks? A parade?"

Meredith shook her head and smiled. "Being a witch is never painful, Alexandra, and hardly as glamorous as fireworks or a parade. You know that."

I nodded slowly. "I know. It's just that losing them was so painful. I guess I expected the same in reverse."

Magma pointed one crooked finger in the air. "Losing your powers is an unnatural act. Therefore, it is painful. Your powers were always meant to be yours, so the process is natural."

"But how am I supposed to know if it worked if I hardly felt anything?"

Blake joined the others as they laughed. "Alex. Just try them."

Right. Good idea. Duh.

I opened the palm of my hand hesitantly. "*What if they never came back? What if I'm not a witch...forever?*"

"*You're a witch, Alex. Trust.*" Blake pushed his thoughts to me. I whipped my head in his direction, eyes wide.

"*I heard your thoughts! I couldn't hear other people's thoughts before. Only Blackjack if he let me...*"

He smiled. *"Looks like you might have a new power— reading people's minds. So here's a thought for you, Alexandra. I love you."*

I beamed at him as tears blurred my vision. *"I love you too, Blake."*

I looked at my hand. A giant ball of golden-white energy burst from my palm...

"Everyone, let's go for a drive," I said, closing my palm and extinguishing the flame.

Blake tilted his head. "Where to?"

"To visit my mom. It's about time you met."

EVERYONE GATHERED around my mother in her room. It was a little crowded, but we all packed in there. We were way over the capacity of people allowed for visiting hours, but passing security was easy.

Hilarious, actually.

We were all vying for who would use magic to trick the guard and scoot a group of witches—seven—a perfect number for a coven, into Mom's room. Teddy wanted to use glamor to disguise us as orderlies. Meredith suggested she cloak us. I insisted we walk in and tell the charge nurse I had family from out of town and this was the only opportunity we'd have to visit Mom.

Magma won.

As we were all arguing and laughing about it outside the building, the little Mage snuck in, tossed a spell this way and that, and motioned for us to join her. We slipped quickly past security, and the duty nurse and I led the way to Mother's room.

I opened the door, shuffling everyone inside. Mom was sitting in her wheelchair in front of the window.

"Eek! The flies!" Teddy shrieked.

A murmur of disturbed voices rippled through the room as we watched the black cloud of hundreds of flies swirling above Mom's head.

"What are those? Why are they there?" Blake asked. I realized this would have been a first for him. The last time he was around, anyone under a demon's curse was in Mitch Myle's cell. Blake wasn't a witch then. Having powers meant you had particular sight, too.

"Those are Sentries, Son," Lucas answered. "A protective swarm, placed by the demon himself, to ensure the victim remains...a victim."

Oblivious to the swarm or the group of people who just entered, Mom sat staring out the window. She was a hollow shell of the mother I knew. I walked over to where she sat in her wheelchair. Kneeling before her, I glanced into her eyes but said nothing. I knew I wouldn't get a response, so I didn't bother trying. Mom's silver hair and blue eyes reflected the winter sun. Once as blue as sparkling oceans, her eyes appeared lifeless and dull.

I hope this works, Mom.

A sudden desperation to see Mom's eyes sparkle again pulsed through me.

Ignoring the swarm, I closed the draperies, softened the light inside the room, pushed Mom's wheelchair into the center of the room, and discussed what to do with the group. Teddy pulled out the candles we had packed and placed them around the room, lighting them. Soon, the room was glowing and warm.

"What have you and Waldo tried previously?" Lucas asked.

On hearing the mention of his name, Cressy's ethereal essence appeared. "You called?"

"Really, Cress? Is it just that easy?" I moaned, recalling all the times I went through grand preparations to summon my mentor when it wasn't necessary.

Cressy smiled. "Hello, dear child. How may I be of assis —oh." He spotted my mother in the center of the room. "Belinda." He nodded toward her. Mom showed no response. Even as a gauzy ghost, I could see Cressy's features shift. His brow furrowed, and he dropped his gaze.

"Waldo," Lucas asked, "I was just asking what you've tried previously—to rid Belinda of the demon's curse."

Cressy pursed his lips and remained silent. I jumped in. "I can answer that, Lucas. Nothing." Lucas's eyebrows shot up. "You see, the demon who put my Mother under this hex is the same demon who killed Cress." Audible gasps came from Teddy, Meredith, and Magma. "I've tried myself, and again with Penny and Teddy, to lift the curse. We brought her out from under for only a few seconds. Cressy insisted it would take more witches—a coven—to do anything effective."

"I see," Lucas answered. "Well, do you have any idea who the demon was?"

"None, I'm afraid." Cressy shook his head, hands clasped behind him. "Perhaps the truth will finally be revealed if you successfully bring Belinda back."

"Can we do that, Dad? Not knowing what we're dealing with?" Blake asked, his brow knitting together.

"Well, we can certainly try. Alexandra, tell me, what spell was so effective last time?"

Teddy piped up. "It was my potion that did the trick! The same potion I used on some gnarly nuns." She pulled a corked vial from her bag and proudly held it up to show everyone.

Lucas's brow shot up. "Oh?"

"It's a long story," I smiled, "But yes, Teddy's potion did the trick. I asked her to recreate it for today, just in case."

"Well, I'm sure it will help." Meredith smiled at Teddy, who proudly stuck out her chin, grinning.

"Malcolm, you've been awfully quiet. Do you have any suggestions?" I asked.

Malcolm's large, prominent features were stern. "I'm sorry for my silence, Alexandra. I didn't realize this was the same demon who killed my brother. The news has me a bit —quiet. I regretfully could not come to Waldo's aid. I was on the other side of the world, battling a rather villainous demon." He glanced at Cressy, who offered a small smile.

"It is okay, my brother. You couldn't have known what would happen. None of us did."

Malcolm's lips pulled into what I would have to consider a smile. "I have a suggestion, however. Lucas, are you familiar with the Elevatio Daemoniorum Maledictio?"

Lucas tapped his forehead with a finger. "I believe I am, although I've never performed it, personally."

"I've never heard of it. What's the meaning?" I asked.

"Translated, it means 'lifting a demon's curse,'" Malcolm answered. "It's quite effective when the demon is of unknown origin."

My hand fluttered to my chest. *Could removing this curse finally be possible?* "Can you teach us, Malcolm?"

"Of course. Does anyone have paper and something to write with?"

"I do." Magma reached into her bag, pulling out tissues, Werther's, her wand, a few random potion bottles, and a small tree frog before coming to a notepad and pen. We all chuckled when the frog started leaping around the room, Teddy squealing, trying to catch it.

Malcolm scribbled the incantation onto six pieces of notepaper, ripped them from the pad, and handed them out.

"Latin?" Blake asked. "I failed Latin in high school."

"You did what?" Lucas and Meredith stared at Blake wide-eyed.

Blake grimaced. We all laughed.

"Ahh, I see." Malcom nodded. "Allow me to interpret. He handed the pen and pad to Blake. Malcolm said the spell in English;

"Gods of the north, south, east, and west, we ask that you grant our request.

Return that which has been suppressed. Release Belinda from this hex."

"Really? That's it?" Blake asked, eyes wide, staring at his notes.

Malcolm nodded. "That's it. But chanted, over and over, with intention. This," Malcolm pointed to the notepad, "along with Teddy's potion, should be sufficient curse removal."

I could barely breathe. Shivers of excited energy coursed through me.

I was about to get my mom back.

Please, please, please let this work.

"Alex? You okay? You're white as a sheet." Blake asked, wrapping an arm around my waist, a look of concern across his handsome features.

A tear slid down my cheek. "Fine, yes. I...I can't believe this is happening. Mom's been gone for...over twenty years.

And now," I looked around the room at the menagerie of witches, "you're all here, making this possible."

Smiling, everyone, including Cressy, surrounded me in a group hug.

My family.

My coven.

"Okay, okay, let's get this curse lifted!" Blake shouted.

We circled Mom's wheelchair once again and held hands. Cressy floated nearby, observing. We started by chanting the incantation repeatedly, the various tones of voices creating a vibration that permeated the room. The wind picked up around the sentry flies, aggravated as the chanting grew more aggressive. I broke away from the circle and brought the vial of Teddy's potion to Mom's lips.

Holding her chin, I tipped her head back while tipping the liquid past her lips. I could feel her throat work as she stared up at me with hollow eyes.

"Hang on, Mom. You'll be with us soon." I whispered, praying to the Goddess that she wouldn't experience any pain.

Returning to my place in the circle, the chanting ensued. Raising our hands in the air, the chanting became louder as we pushed our intentions toward Mom. Once a tight cyclone above Mom's head, the flies buzzed, dispersing around the room, some hitting us in the face or around our ears to force us to stop, but we continued, matching their aggression.

A low moan escaped Mom's lips. Everyone's heads whipped toward her but continued the chanting. Her moans grew louder and louder, her eyes bulging, staring at nothing, but grew wider as though she'd just seen something horrifying. With one loud moan, she threw her head back and opened her mouth.

Thousands of flies burst forth, scattering into the room and swirling around us. We were all swatting at them; mouths closed as they attempted to fly into any open orifice.

"Keep chanting!" Lucas yelled, then coughed out a fly.

We did so, somewhat broken as we were being attacked by the flies that seemed to pour out of my Mother in an endless stream. We chanted louder and louder, forcibly attempting to overpower the demonic flies with our spell.

It was working.

When the final fly was released, Mom's mouth snapped shut, and she stared straight at me.

The flies that had dispersed suddenly vanished. A calm hush fell over the room.

"Mom? Mom!" I rushed to her, kneeling in front of her. Grasping her head in both hands, I turned her to face me. "Mom, can you hear me? It's Alexandra. Mom!" The room fell silent as the coven grew closer, tightening the circle and watching us. "Mom, please, can you hear me?" I stared at her lifeless eyes as tears trickled down my cheeks.

Nothing.

Mom stared, as she always had, straight ahead.

I released her face and, covering my face with my hands, laid my head on her lap and sobbed.

I cried, letting it all out. All the pain and frustration of never winning the battle against the demon who had suppressed my mother so long ago. I cried for all the years I'd missed having her around to love and be loved. I cried because Mom would never be part of my new family and know what it would be like to live in the new world.

When I thought I couldn't shed another tear, I felt a warm hand stroking my head, and a gasp fluttered around the room.

"Alexandra?"

I sniffed. Wiping my eyes, I looked up.

My Mother's beautiful, sparkling blue eyes were looking down on me.

"Mommy?"

"Hello, sweetheart. It's so good to see you again."

EPILOGUE

SIX MONTHS LATER

On the eve of the summer solstice—Litha—spring flowers were no longer a promise of warm weather to come; they were in full bloom. The scent of Yarrow, Larkspur, and Peonies from my bouquet clung to the fresh sea air. Everyone we knew, old friends and new—witches out from under the eternal darkness of hiding—were in attendance.

Blackjack, begrudgingly wearing a collar of lavender around his neck, slowly paced in front of me, two small gold rings tied by a white ribbon tinkling together as he walked.

The salty air clung to my skin, my long dark hair whipping in the wind as I took slow steps forward, my mother at my side. My simple, white peasant dress blew back and forth with every kiss of the ocean breeze.

The crown of lavender encircling my head, matching the small bouquet of lavender in my hand, released a steady scent as the wind whirled around us. It calmed as I stepped closer to the altar, set against the ocean backdrop in the backyard of my home on Ocean View Drive.

And stepped closer to Blake.

Dressed in an equally simple white linen shirt, a sprig of lavender pinned over his heart and the scar left by Murder's blade, Blake's hair, kept long despite his sheriff's uniform requirements, touched the base of his neck. His neat beard was trimmed for the occasion. His deep brown eyes danced in the sunset's glow.

I turned to Mom, her light blue eyes sparkling and curly silver hair in place, thanks to an entire bottle of hairspray. Her simple linen suit, a particular favorite from the clothes I kept for her, was just a touch baggy on her older, slender frame. She had lost a lot of weight while at Lexington but gained some back with love and home cooking.

"Love you, Mom."

"Love you, dear." I leaned over to kiss her cheek—left, then right—before she took my hand and Blakes into hers, kissing them both and joining them together.

I gazed into Blake's eyes and returned his welcoming smile. His hand felt warm; a surge of energy poured from his hand into mine and rode up my arm straight to my heart.

I breathed deeply as Penny, our self-appointed officiant, began.

"Friends and witches, we gather on this eve, at the edge of this world and the next, to witness the union of two super-awesome peeps I'm blessed to call my family." A course of giggles rose from the small gathering. "We stand where flesh and magic meet, in the company of friends and spirits. That's you, Cressy." Penny nodded toward Cressy as he brushed a ghostly tear from his gauzy cheeks and smiled.

"We are here to cast a bond between Blake and Alexandra for all eternity. A bond that even death won't break. Do the two of you," she nodded toward us, "each take the other on this occasion and forever?"

"We do." Blake and I spoke in unison.

"As spring brings the freshness of life anew, the promise of summer and its bright bounty lies around the corner. We are part of the natural world. Our seasons are brief, but where the physical plane gives way to spirit, love moves like breath." Penny smiled proudly. "I wrote that. Pretty good, huh?" Laughter filled the salt air.

"That was great, Pen," I whispered.

"I know, right?" She whispered back. Penny bound Blake's and my hands with a cord of sweetgrass. "Love, woven in the wind, is unending. Eternal." She said as she bound us together with a Celtic knot. She held our bound hands in hers. "Are you ready to marry?"

I glanced at Blake and smiled. "Yes."

He smiled back. "Aye."

"Then let us cast the spell. Repeat after me." Penny made an animated throat-clearing noise.

"Heart bound to heart...and soul bound to soul... I am my own... but also yours... Our union grows...of kindness, caring... trust well-deserved...and love unerring. Heart bound to heart...and soul to soul bound. This love is eternal, our love unending."

As Blake and I repeated after Penny, the glow in my heart burned with the promise of what was to come and what had already arrived.

Our future as witches in a world without Witch Hunters was our new reality. Witches could move about freely and embrace their true nature without fear of persecution.

My mother was out from a demon's curse, healthy and

healing, and living with Blake and me in the home she raised me in. We spent our days talking about the parts of my life that she missed while she was away, and she happily went to work every day at the apothecary, helping Teddy create products that didn't require magic.

Because Mom wasn't a witch.

Never had been.

She fell in love with my father, a witch and Dagon ancestor, who took his own life to protect ours.

Although I have tried to connect with him in the beyond since Mom's awakening, neither Cressy nor I have been able to. We must assume he is far up in the ethers, unwilling to show himself, but I would continue trying.

At least until—one day—I joined them both on the other side.

Until then, there were things to manage here. There were still angry hunters to tame, potions to create, covens to form, and the occasional demon to fight.

Embracing my role as High Priestess and with Blake at my side, I knew there was nothing we couldn't conquer.

Together.

WHAT'S NEXT?

"Origins" is a Castle Point Witch Series prequel!

You can order here!

"Join Alexandra and Penny when, as young witches, they come into their powers, fighting against their alternate-reality world and their need to be accepted by their peers—including Blake. Find out why Alexandra spent time in Juvenile detention, how Belinda fell under a demon's curse, and how Cressy was killed in "Origins. A Castle Point Witch Series Prequel"

For more books, please visit https://tammytyreebooks. com/

If you enjoyed this book, please leave a review on your favorite platform or on my website here: https://www. tammytyree.com/reviews

Don't miss out on a single new release, discount, offers, and more!!

Sign up, and we'll ensure you hear about every new book Tammy Tyree publishes as soon as it hits the stores. https://forms.wix.com/f/7059185095252377682

Want to read as Tammy writes? Join her membership here https://reamstories.com/tammytyree/public and be the FIRST to read, participate in character and story development, covers and more!

If you found spelling mistakes or niggly plot points, or you'd like to join my ARC/Beta Reader group, please email the author directly: tammy@tammytyree.com

ALSO BY TAMMY TYREE

Fiction:

The Castle Point Witch Series

https://tammytyreebooks.com/collections/castle----point----witch----series

Coming Soon:

The Corpse Collector Cozy Mystery Series

"Welcome to the "Corpse Collector Paranormal Women's Fiction Cozy Mystery Series," starring Carrigan, a sassy 40-something body removal expert. She's not just wrangling bodies at Castle Point Funeral Home; she's also juggling chatty ghosts helping crack the cases of their demises. With humor as her sidekick, Carrigan unravels mysteries while keeping the afterlife laugh-out-loud lively."

Non—Fiction

"Dead Men Still Snore; A Woman's True Story of Love, Loss, and Channeling her Husband's Messages from the Other Side."

FOR AUTHORS

Are you an author, looking to up-level your career, your writing, or your time? The Author Revolution Academy has everything you need to succeed!**

Aspiring & Emerging Author Courses

Are you working toward getting your very first book out? Maybe you have a small (but growing backlist of titles)... If so, look no further. These courses are the best fit for you.

The Story Cure: http://bit.ly/410XVqW

Plan Your Series Challenge: http://bit.ly/3GFAv27

Indie Publishing Fundamentals: http://bit.ly/3GDrd6W

Prolific Author Course

Ready to take self-publishing to the next level? Rapid Release Roadmap is the course to get it done. Learn how to plan, write, publish, and promote 4 books (or more) every single year in this one-of-a-kind course!

Rapid Release Road Map: http://bit.ly/3o8b8zu

Millionaire Author Courses

Want to learn how to apply the Law of Attraction and manifestation techniques to your author career? Look no further! These courses (or membership) are just what you're looking for!

Millionaire Author Challenge: http://bit.ly/43osfNP

Millionaire Author Manifestation: http://bit.ly/3KoY5RQ

Abundant Author Activation: http://bit.ly/3MA2Iew

**Affiliate links

ABOUT THE AUTHOR

Tammy Tyree is a retired Board Certified Clinical Hypnotherapist and award-winning author of paranormal suspense and memoir.

Most of her professional career was dealing with entity attachments and demonic possession, which she thought was rather fun. Now, she works alongside International Bestselling author Carissa Andrews to up-level the lives of aspiring authors to manifest millionaire author careers.

She has four adult children and one incredibly perfect granddaughter she regularly sees and spoils.

You can follow Tammy on Facebook and Instagram, and visit her website at www.tammytyreebooks.com

Book an "Inner Light Insight" Hypnotherapy / Psychic Session with Tammy! https://tammytyree.com

"Discover. Heal. Empower. Illuminate Your Path Within."

An Inner Light Insight session is a transformative 60-minute experience that blends the power of Hypnotherapy, Reiki, Energy Work, Tarot, Channeling, and more. This session will guide you on a holistic journey of self-discovery, healing, and empowerment.

Tammy is dedicated to helping you tap into your inner wisdom and unlock your full potential. Whether seeking personal growth, spiritual guidance, or a path to inner peace, our tailored sessions are thoughtfully crafted to illuminate the path to your true self.

Inner Light Insight

ILLUMINATE YOUR PATH WITHIN

facebook.com/tammytyreebooks

instagram.com/tammytyreeauthor

tiktok.com/@authortammytyree

goodreads.com/22262505.Tammy_Tyree

bookbub.com/authors/tammy-tyree

amazon.com/author/Tammy-Tyree